S0-AXQ-718

GOSHEN PUBLIC LIBRARY
601 SOUTH FIFTH STREET
DISCARDED 46526-3994

# STEALING
# APRIL'S HEART

GOSHEN PUBLIC LIBRARY
601 SOUTH FIFTH STREET
DISCARDED
GOSHEN, IN 46526-3994

# STEALING
# APRIL'S HEART

•

## Kathryn Quick

*AVALON BOOKS*
NEW YORK

© Copyright 2003 by Kathryn Quick
Library of Congress Catalog Card Number: 2002093582
ISBN 0-8034-9573-0
All rights reserved.
All the characters in this book are fictitious,
and any resemblance to actual persons,
living or dead, is purely coincidental.
Published by Thomas Bouregy & Co., Inc.
160 Madison Avenue, New York, NY 10016

PRINTED IN THE UNITED STATES OF AMERICA
ON ACID-FREE PAPER
BY HADDON CRAFTSMEN, BLOOMSBURG, PENNSYLVANIA

## FOR MOM

and thanks to Christine J., Irene, Anne, Chris R., Ronnie and Mary for their expertise and support.

## Chapter One

April Stevens sat behind her walnut desk paging through the contents of a manila folder containing a man's life.

Ryne Anderson, age 31. All-Star third baseman for the New York Rockets. Protocols attached for fast-tracked rehabilitation after repair of tear to right medial meniscus with some secondary damage to the anterior curciate ligament. Evaluation and conclusion in four months.

It said so little and yet, so much. April's trained eye could see exactly what the slips of papers were really saying. Six weeks after the arthroscopic surgery, Ryne Anderson was a sports casualty, and as a casualty, those in charge were filing him away until a definite decision could be made on his physical condition.

She flipped through the folder and found nothing remarkable about his case. There were no other notes, no personal recommendations, and no indications to Ander-

1

son's disposition or state of mind, only the implication in black and white on lab reports and physical examinations. Underneath the roar of the fans and the glory of the game, baseball is a business and as a business, production counted. Over the next few weeks she and the staff of Princeton Sports Medicine would decide if Ryne Anderson would be physically able to produce in time for the next baseball season.

The aggressive therapy needed to get him back before spring training would be a daunting task for even a larger, well-established rehabilitation clinic. For April, while she refused to consider the possibility it would be impossible, she had to admit it would be a formidable challenge.

April opened Princeton Sports Medicine three years ago with only a dream and the financial help of a family friend. Family and friends cautioned her about the gamble it might be for a woman to venture out into the largely male territory of sports medicine, but the hard work was finally beginning to pay off. This past year, the clinic seemed to be turning the corner as its reputation began to spread through the sporting ranks. A few local professional teams were finally giving her clinic a try.

A few more successes like the quarterback from the New York Giants who came in for an injury to the elbow on his throwing arm, or the hockey player from the Devils who had back damage from a nasty hip check, and she could repay the loan for the sizable start-up costs. Then she could begin to think more about expanding the services to help the people in the community who couldn't normally afford the programs she offered. That was a big part of her dream—that's why Ryne Anderson was so important.

He'd suffered a pretty serious post-season injury, and it would test her skills to the limit to get him back in his ball club's line-up by spring training in March. If it all worked out, however, the clinic would be firmly set on the road to success.

Daydreaming about the additional staff she'd have to hire to handle the increased business, April jumped in her chair when a voice swept the pleasant picture of the future from her mind.

"Our star's here." Jenny Cole, one of the clinic's staff members and also April's friend, peeked in from the doorway. "I haven't actually seen him, but he's supposed to be a real hunk," she added with a gleam in her eye. "And I hear he is as talented off the field as he is on it. Supposed to have a smile that can melt ice. And eyes that—"

"Enough, Jen." April said quickly. "You know how important this case is."

Jenny closed the door behind her and sat down in the chair facing April. "Thinking about the future again?"

April nodded. "More than thinking about it now." She clenched her fists and pounded the air. "If I can pull this off . . ." She stopped. Determination set her chin at an unwavering angle. "No, I mean *when* I pull this off and send Anderson back to his team, I may be able to open up the satellite office in New York we talked about. Once we get more exposure and a firm footing on the East Coast, we can start accepting kids who otherwise might not get a second chance."

"Nice thought, but it'll cost big bucks to do that."

"Which brings us back to now. Here. The starting point."

Jenny shook her head. "I don't know how you stay so focused. Put me in a room full of gorgeous semi-clad men flexing their pecs and I'd be tempted to illustrate a few sports moves of my own."

Amused, April grinned. "It seems I have to keep reminding you that our clients are here to regain the pinnacle of fitness to enhance their job performance and not to audition for a potential relationship."

"A potential relationship is something you could use."

April quirked her eyebrows. "Oh really?"

"Yes, really."

Propping her chin in her hand, April tried to look casual. "First, I get this place out of the red, then I worry about relationships."

"Not a problem." Jenny snapped her fingers in the air. "Marry your investor, that rich guy from New England. I bet he'd cancel the loan as a wedding present."

"Sorry, I don't work that way." April shook her head and swiveled in the chair. "And neither does Wil Tyler. He considers the Center a good investment. I intend to pay back every penny plus interest. There's nothing hidden or covert about his involvement with this place or with me. It's strictly a business relationship in both areas."

"Are you sure?"

"Positive."

"Too bad. It could work out." Jenny got up and walked around the desk to face April. Grabbing the arm of the chair, she pushed it hard and then pulled April to her feet. "Look at you. Gorgeous auburn hair, green eyes that could put jade to shame, great body, probably from all those aerobics classes you take and teach, and worse than that, you're actually nice. You'd make the perfect socialite for the New England upper crust."

"I don't want to be a socialite. I want to be the owner of the best sports therapy center in the country."

"Success takes time in this business."

April adjusted her smile. "So you never fail to remind me. But seriously, it has been a long day and before I get to Ryne Anderson, I have to deal with Kevin Johnson."

"Bummer. What's the prognosis on the kid?"

April bit down on her bottom lip. "I'm afraid the season is over for him. There's a lot of hard work ahead if he's even going to get that arm strong enough to think about next year. It's going to be difficult to tell him. He's only twelve. Pretty young to understand that if he doesn't put his whole heart into his therapy, any kind of ball playing just might be out for good." April felt her face tighten with familiar pain. "This is the only part of running this place I actually hate."

"Can I help?"

"No, I need to do this." April sighed and summoned up the strength she usually reserved for this kind of news. "Kevin's mom told me that every time he sees a doctor in the room, he freaks out."

"He's probably afraid one of them is going to end his budding career."

"Apparently. Then right after Kevin, Ryne Anderson is my last appointment. Where is he?"

"I think he's downstairs in the weight room. On tour." Jenny took a few steps toward the door and stopped. "Oh, when you see him, get me a pass to opening day at City Stadium, will you?"

"You can probably get it yourself. We both know you have your eye on that relief pitcher who's here for rehab after rotator-cuff surgery."

Jenny waved off April's remark as she left. Then in another second, she popped her head back in the room. "I almost forgot to tell you, I put the updated information you wanted on isokenetic testing on your desk."

"Thanks," April called out before settling back down and picking up the Anderson folder. Rocking back and forth in the chair, she paged again through the report from the staff orthopedist, Dr. McKee.

Ryne Anderson's injury would require a tough weight routine to strengthen the muscles around the kneecap along with a program to build flexibility and agility. After she spoke to Anderson, she'd send him downstairs for a final range of motion and strength test. Anderson was already four weeks into rehab and the reports suggested he could start a graduated return to athletics. Then just as soon as she got the test results, she'd sit down with Dr. McKee and the Rockets' team physician and map out a plan to do just that.

The file skidded across the desktop when she tossed it down. This was going to be a tricky one. She got up and walked out to Jenny's desk and riffled through the data on isokenetics. She would need all the information she could get her hands on to make it all work.

If it was going to work at all.

\* \* \*

"So, how's the knee?" Roger Taylor, Ryne's teammate and designated cohabitant while Ryne was in the therapy program in Princeton, stopped tugging on a set of weights. He wiped away some perspiration from his forehead with a towel before joining his fellow Rocket near the door.

Ryne shrugged. "Okay. It's been four weeks so we're kicking the rehab into high gear. How's the arm?"

"Great." Roger slapped his left hand on his right shoulder and did some arm circles. "First time all year I can do this without pain. I'm getting stronger all the time, too." He flexed his arm at the elbow a few times. "Had the fastball clocked at seventy miles per hour yesterday just throwing softly. Should be back up to speed and ready to pitch by March." He reached back down and began to lift.

Ryne looked around. "Are you happy rehabbing here?"

Roger steadied the barbell as it bounced to a stop on the floor. "Sure, it's great."

Everything suddenly came together and weighed down on Ryne. "I think I'd be more comfortable in New York, but I'm not paying the tab." He looked around the small weight room as Roger walked over to the hand weights and the obvious looked back at him. This was undoubtedly going to be the worst few months of his life. "Distractions," Ryne muttered under his breath.

Roger glanced at Ryne using the mirrors hung on the wall. "Huh? You talkin' to me?"

Waving Roger off with an anxious swipe of one hand, Ryne's voice suggested displeasure. "Ah, I was sent here so I could concentrate on coming back to full strength without the media nosing around. The team doctor said there'd be less distractions here." He pushed his bottom lip forward in thought. "You know, Rog, I'm really starting to hate that word."

"Have you seen the place's owner?" Roger asked casually.

Ryne slouched back onto the wall and folded his arms in front of his chest. "Not yet. But I have an appointment with him soon. What on earth does that have to do with my training?"

"So you haven't met the boss yet."

Ryne wrinkled his eyebrows. "No, why?"

"Just curious." Roger loved to keep people off balance. Psychedelic conversation, he liked to call it.

Ryne strode over to his friend and stood nose to nose with him. "I recognize that look. You know something."

"You were probably too busy handing out autographs to notice the picture on the wall of the ribbon cutting for this place when you came in, but he's a she."

"She," Ryne sputtered, shaking his head and chalking another strike against this whole idea. "You mean my trainer is a woman?"

"Far as I can tell without touching."

"Very funny," Ryne replied, sarcasm lacing his voice. "Playing ball is my life. I need the best to help make sure I'm back by the spring."

"Hit a sore spot, did I?" Roger said with a smile. "So you haven't met her yet?"

"No, but I'll bet she's a muscular chick who looks like a linebacker." Ryne found no confirmation or denial in Roger's body language.

"I think you'd better check this one out for yourself."

Ryne rolled his eyes and let out an exasperated sigh. "One less distraction at least." The frown on his face suddenly turned itself upside down as he watched a tall blond woman enter the room and extend her hand toward him.

"Hello, Mr. Anderson, I'm Jennifer Cole. Miss Stevens would like you to go right up to her office as soon as you're through here."

"Why, hello," he said, taking her hand in his right and covering it with his left. "Please. Call me Ryne." The light of his smile could have powered Princeton for a month.

"Well then, Ryne," Jenny said without rancor, pulling her hand free and noticing that the grapevine had been right about his smile, "take the elevator to the top floor. It's the last office on the left."

"Are you my therapist?"

"Sorry, no."

"Too bad. You'd be a nice . . ." he looked at Roger and winked, ". . . distraction." Roger rolled his eyes to the ceiling and shook his head.

Jenny quickly caught the veiled implication. "Sorry, again, but I don't do diversions."

"I know a brush-off when I'm handed one." Ryne cocked his thumb to the ceiling. "Top floor and last office on the right?" When Jenny nodded, he moved his hand in a salute and headed toward the elevator.

"You've gotta watch him," Roger said, giving Jenny an affectionate peck on the cheek. "He's smooth."

"Well, the only thing that's going to be smooth about him here, will be his movements in my aerobics class." She thumped him on the arm. "Back to work. We have a date later and I want you in top physical shape for it."

The elevator on the top floor opened to the sound of a light scuffle and running footsteps coming in Ryne's direction as he exited the car.

"Stop him," a clearly female voice called out just as a boy Ryne guessed was about twelve or thirteen zipped by him like a shot.

Taking two long strides, Ryne caught up with the youth and grabbed onto his shirt with one hand. "Whoa, what's the hurry?" he asked about the same time as he noticed the large cast on the boy's left arm. He motioned to it with his free hand. "Broken?"

The boy squirmed against Ryne's grip. "Lemme go."

April caught up to the pair a moment later. "Thanks. Kevin here was trying to make a fast getaway, and—"

As she spoke, she looked from Kevin's face up into Ryne's and the most remarkable thing happened, something that never happened to her before. When their eyes met, her mind went blank, absolutely empty. Gone were all thoughts of training programs and rehab regimes, replaced instead by fascination with the most incredible pair of brown eyes she had ever seen. Above them a stray lock of sandy hair tumbled down onto the man's forehead, giving him a playful, boyish look, the kind of look that makes a woman want to reach out and brush the hair back off his face and away from his eyes. The smile that played off those eyes told her that, if first impressions were truly lasting impressions, this one was going with her to the grave.

"And," she continued with a barely perceptible shake of her head to get her speech center going again, "I think Kevin could have outrun me to the door." She motioned to his sneakers and her heels. "He definitely has an edge in the footwear department."

By this time, Kevin had finished trying to get free. He jerked his head up, determined, defiant and ready to fight, when he suddenly realized who was holding him captive. "Hey, you're Ryne Anderson. Wow! What are you doing here?"

Ryne Anderson, April repeated inside her mind. So this is our star. A mighty good-looking one at that, she noted. The wayward thought danced inside her head before she had a chance to corral it and send it packing. She prided herself on being able to keep her feminine response apart from her clinical reaction and wasn't about to let things get out of hand now. As a rule, when a woman ventured out into a man's world like sports, she was bound to come in contact with some good-looking men. She knew how to handle that little detail, had handled it a few times successfully before.

Still, this one, with his sandy hair, square chin and warm brown eyes that she didn't doubt for one minute could really melt ice, left her practically speechless with just one look. Dealing with a gym full of men on a daily basis normally never affected her that way. But this one had, and they really hadn't even formally been introduced. It was time to get back on track. Fast.

"Mr. Anderson is here to get his knee back into shape," April said, keeping her features deceptively composed. "Just like you're here to get your arm in shape, Kevin."

The words caused Kevin to forget his hero for the moment. "It's never gonna be right. You said so."

"What I said was, it's not going to come back in time for this season." April looked over at Ryne, who was staring at the white cast. "Kevin shattered his arm when he lost control of his bike and hit a tree. He has a lot of hard work ahead of him if he wants to play ball again. When he will, however, is partly up to him."

The boy looked up at Ryne, his eyes icing over with controlled tears. "It's my pitching arm. Tell her, Mr. Anderson, tell her what it means when you can't play ball anymore."

Ryne let go of Kevin's arm and struggled with how to respond. Lifting his eyes, he looked over at April who pressed her lips together, raising her eyebrows in a silent plea. Fortunately, Ryne read her body language loud and clear.

He wanted to do it right. It was an important decision for anyone to make, at any age. If he could, he would have dropped down on one knee to emphasize the message he was about to deliver, but he couldn't risk straining his own injury any further.

"Listen, kid—" he began, putting both hands on Kevin's shoulders and looking him right in the eye.

"His name is Kevin," April gently reminded Ryne.

Ryne nodded. "Look, Kevin. Plenty of guys sit out one season with injuries and then knock 'em dead the next. It's what you do with the time off that makes the difference."

Kevin dropped his head and dug the tip of one shoe into the tiled floor. "I know."

"Well, the way I see it, you and I are in the same boat and we have two options. We can sit around and feel sorry for ourselves, or, we can tough it out and fight back."

Kevin kicked at the floor again and seemed to be trying to sort out his options. Suddenly, he jerked his head up and shot questions at Ryne in rapid-fire fashion. As Ryne tried to answer each one, April stepped back.

She tried to keep an open mind and not stereotype when she had accepted the assignment on Ryne Anderson. What she knew about him, she only knew from headlines in the papers and stories in *Sports Illustrated*. He certainly didn't appear to be as arrogant as the media painted him on paper and right now she hoped he actually believed in some of the things that he was telling Kevin about courage and hard work.

Sudden shivers shot through her as she listened to him speak. He was beginning to sound too much like someone else who had tried to come back after an injury, but had failed. Her brother, Rob, one of her main reasons for starting this clinic.

Rob was a promising athlete who lived and breathed football when they were growing up right up until the time an injury cut his career short. If she learned anything by what happened to Rob, she learned that athletes who lived and breathed their careers tended to crumble when the setbacks started piling up. And since opening the clinic, she never went through one rehab program that didn't have its share of stumbling blocks.

"Well, Kevin, that's the bottom line," she heard Ryne say, his words pulling her out of her memories. "Which will it be?"

Kevin looked over at his arm and then up at Ryne. "Aw, I guess I could try it."

April noticed Ryne's face suddenly set, his mouth tighten, his eyes fix on something inside his own mind. "There is no try," he said. "You just do it." There was an edge to his voice, one that spoke of apprehensions. Quickly he changed his tone. "Tell you what, my first day back in uniform, you can be guest ball boy for the team."

Kevin suddenly forgot all about his arm. "Wow, promise!"

"Promise." Ryne answered with a wink.

April smiled. She arched an arm around Kevin's shoulders and steered him toward the elevator. "Now," she said, "down to Dr. McKee's office. Your parents are there now, picking up your schedule. You know where it is, don't you?"

"Yeah." Kevin stopped in his tracks and raised his arm. "But sign my cast first, Mr. Anderson?"

Ryne reached in his inside coat pocket for a pen. "My pleasure, son. On one condition—that you remember me when you win the Cy Young Award for pitching in a few years."

When the signature was properly in place and Kevin was on his way downstairs, Ryne and April began to walk toward her office.

"Thanks for the words of encouragement," April said. "Just before he whizzed out of the office, Kevin had all but decided to quit baseball for good."

"The scouts predict a shortage of left-handed pitchers over the next few years. Can't let a good prospect slip by."

Even though the situation wasn't quite as dramatic as his own retirement would be, Ryne could sympathize with the way Kevin was feeling right about now. He brushed it back to the recesses of his mind.

When April looked into Ryne's eyes, for a moment, she saw fear. But it vanished almost as quickly as it appeared. "Whatever your reason is, thanks. I don't think I could have caught him. You saved my life." She saw a twinkle of amusement brighten the gold in his eyes.

"I try to make it a point of knowing whose life I save."

By this time they were in front of her office. April tapped her knuckles on the nameplate. "Hers."

Ryne raised an eyebrow. "So you're the coach."

"You bet." April pushed opened the door and motioned for Ryne to go inside. "Make yourself comfortable, Mr. Anderson. Your coach is about to fill you in on the ground rules." She walked around the desk, slid open its top drawer, and took out a file folder about two inches thick.

While April again leafed through pages and pages of reports, Ryne took the time to take a quick look around. The room smelled of lemon furniture polish with just the faint touch of good perfume.

Then he took stock of the woman who owned it all and liked what he saw. It wasn't only the way she looked that intrigued him. True, it was human nature for a man to notice an attractive woman, especially one as appealing as April, but there was something more to this one. Style, maybe. Or confidence. Maybe her trying to make it in a man's field brought out a confidence that had its own style. Whatever it was, he would definitely take the time to try to find out over the coming weeks.

"First and foremost," April began, "is that you put one hundred and fifty percent into your rehab or else . . ." Her voice trailed off. Ryne was staring at her. "Questions?"

"Just a comment."

"Shoot."

"You're a cute one, aren't you, coach?"

April just barely caught herself before her mouth fell open. She never thought of herself as cute. She thought of herself as competent.

"Expertly qualified to handle your rehab, you mean. I have a Masters in Physical Therapy from Rutgers University and I make sure I keep up on the latest techniques and trends in rehabilitation." She raised her hand and gestured to the numerous certificates and diplomas hanging on the wall alongside the rich walnut bookcase that was jammed with reference books to emphasize her point. "In addition, I have some of the top orthopedists and therapists on staff led by Aaron McKee, in my opinion, the finest orthopedic surgeon on the East Coast. Are we clear on that?"

"If I have any other questions, I'll ask."

"You do that. And if you want affidavits of a few success stories, I can get those for you, too." She leveled a calm, unblinking stare at him to show she meant it. "But I think you'll be able to judge that for yourself as you progress here."

"You have to admit, it is unusual for a woman to run a sports clinic. Working with you is going to take some getting used to." Leaving it at that, Ryne wasn't about to explain he didn't exactly know which way he meant it, professionally or personally. Despite the team doctor's theory, he had just run into one mighty big distraction.

"Why? Does it matter if your trainer is a man or woman, as long as you get well?" April challenged.

"Guess not."

"Absolutely not. Let me remind you, Mr. Anderson, muscles and ligaments don't come in pink for girls or blue for boys."

Ryne winced. "Sorry, I didn't mean it the way it sounded."

A flush spread across Ryne's cheeks, softening his face and April's anger. It wasn't often she saw a man blush when he was wrong. Maybe she was just being a bit too sensitive. Her voice softened just a bit. "I understand. It is hard to communicate well with one's foot in one's mouth."

The color on Ryne's cheeks brightened to red. "I still need to see what you've got before I'm convinced. I want you to understand that I need to be back in that line-up by spring training."

April extended her hand. "And believe me, Mr. Anderson, I want you there."

As Ryne's large hand took hers, the jolt of contact moved up her arm and into her chest. His touch was firm but tender, sending a tingling down her spine. Strange, she thought, as another vibration moved up her back, I must be coming down with the flu or something.

Ryne felt it, too. He began to smile slowly, the angles of his face shifting and softening as the smile spread. He resisted the urge to use his other hand to smooth her cheek and instead simply said, "Together, how can we miss?"

April forced herself to concentrate on his words and not his touch. "Welcome to Princeton Sports Medicine, then. I guess this means we're going to be working together for a while."

"April," he said, enjoying the way her name sounded, "I'm looking forward to it."

April watched Ryne until he disappeared inside the elevator. Already she could tell that he was a complex man. She shook her head and walked back to the desk. Then sliding his file across the desk toward her, she tapped it thoughtfully with a forefinger.

There was something different about this one. The macho façade he had put on didn't quite seem genuine. Although the room had been filled with the power of his presence, his eyes showed her other things. In them she saw glimpses of determination, propriety, and even fear. And it was the fear that confused her the most. Was he trying to convince Kevin that the rehab program would work and to give it every chance, or was he trying to convince himself?

She picked up the file and read as she paced the room. She hoped to find something she overlooked; something, anything, no matter how tiny that might give her a better sense of the man. But there was still nothing there.

A rush of warmth flashed over her as she realized that this one meeting with Ryne had totally engrossed her in his case. Even if he was intriguing, the timing was all wrong. It was probably all Jenny's talk about relationships soaking into her brain and turning it to mush. She spun around, banging her thigh on the corner of her desk as she tossed the file on the top. As she tried to rub the sting out, she realized Ryne was going to be a problem. She had never been this unsettled by a client before. It had to stop. He could be no different than any of the other athletes at the Center. They would have to work together in a professional way for the good of both his career and her dream.

That was simply the way it was going to be.

The elevator door opened on the bottom level and Ryne exchanged places in the car with Roger. Roger put a finger to the "door open" button. "How'd it go?"

"The lady's definitely not a linebacker."

"Don't get any ideas. You're here to fix the knee, not get fixed up with the trainer."

"Maybe I can do both."

"What, and disappoint half the women in America, Mr. Heartthrob? Besides, from what I see, April Stevens is a professional, smart enough not to mix business and pleasure. This one is out of your league, Anderson." Roger took his hand from the button and made the instantly recognizable "yer out" gesture. "I warn you, it'll be instant ejection from the game if you try it."

"Wait, what do you mean?" Ryne barely got the words out before the elevator doors shut, leaving him, hand in the air, mouth open, talking to polished gray metal. The only answer to his question was the whine of the cable as it raised the car from the basement workout area to ground level.

## Chapter Two

A hand reached around from behind April and snatched the gym bag from the trunk of her car.

"Let me get that for you."

She turned in time to see Ryne sling the bag over his shoulder. It had been nearly a week since she ran into him in the hallway near her office. He was dressed in a Rockets T-shirt and a pair of gray sweatpants. And he looked great in them. "Thanks, but I could have managed," she said, slamming the trunk shut.

"I don't doubt that. I was just resurrecting chivalry."

"So you think it's dead, then?" April replied, as they walked through the parking lot toward the Center.

"Or dormant."

"How's the knee?" Perhaps it was the slight limp that caused April to sweep his length from head to toe, but more likely it was because of the vibrations that moved along her nerves every time she looked at him. It was unnerving, being this drawn to someone she hardly knew.

"Feels good today," he replied.

"I don't remember you being on the schedule. What are you doing here?"

They waited for a car to pass. "I'm taking a low-impact aerobics class. I want to keep my energy up."

"I haven't checked this week's iso-test, but I'm guessing the hamstring/quad analysis has gone over seventy percent of the values for your other leg."

Again Ryne reached around her, this time to open the front door. "Dr. McKee told me that I could begin functional progression if I take it easy for a while. He's scheduled me for some agility drills and . . ." He stopped and turned in response to a voice calling out April's name. He saw her wave. "Who's the suit?" he asked, still holding open the front door and watching an impeccably dressed man approach them at a crisp pace. The dark navy blazer with a logo near the pocket and tan colored pants screamed classic; a look Ryne didn't go for at all.

"Wil Tyler," she replied.

"Who's he?" As the man got closer, Ryne studied him from his traditional haircut to his brown leather shoes.

"A friend of mine from New England."

"How good a friend?"

April glanced at Ryne out of the corner of her eye as she watched Wil approach them. "Very good."

"So you like nerds, then?" Ryne baited, knowing she'd have no time to respond before Tyler caught up to them.

April gave Ryne a scathing look before turning her attention to Wil. "You're early," she said, rising to tiptoes and planting a noisy kiss on his cheek. "You weren't due here for another few hours."

Wil brushed a piece of lint from his jacket. "Caught an early train."

"The Beemer in the shop?" Ryne quipped, checking out the shine on Tyler's designer shoes and the razor edges on his pants.

April shifted, making sure her elbow caught Ryne in his side. "He owns a Jaguar." She turned and smiled. "Wil, this is Ryne Anderson. I've told you about him."

"Yes," Will said with a touch of Massachusetts in his voice, "the baseball player with the bad leg." He extended his hand.

"Knee, actually," Ryne corrected. He clamped down hard on Wil's hand, noticing the gold signet ring Wil had on his finger fold under into his palm. "But she didn't tell me anything about you." He felt a satisfied smirk curl his lips when Tyler grimaced in response to the intensity of the handshake.

With a tug, Will pulled his hand free. He flexed his fingers, otherwise ignoring Ryne. "Darling, I found the perfect desk for your office at Benninger's. I'd like you to come and look at it."

"I told you, I love my desk, Wil. I don't want a new one."

"It's not just any desk, it's a very special desk. It was originally owned by one of the Kennedys."

"I really don't like antiques."

"You'll learn to, darling. I have every confidence in you."

"Hey, go look at the thing," Ryne offered. "What can it hurt?"

April stiffened her back, clicked her teeth together, and gave Ryne a tight-lipped smile. "I'm a Republican."

Will seemed oblivious to the exchange. "Then I thought we could take in an earlier dinner at the Club before sailing to the Vineyard."

"I'll make you a deal," she announced, spinning to fully face Wil. "I'll look at your desk if you agree that for every hour I spend in the antique shop listening to the history of cherry wood and tales of every scratch on the darn thing, you'll spend a hour in my gym."

A long silence followed, then a chuckle came, more patronizing than humorous. "Now, April, you know I'm not one of your sweaty jocks. I never pretended to be. I leave that physical stuff to you."

April felt her nostrils flare. "Fine. Let me carry you to your car and we'll be off. On the way we can stop at the hardware store and pick up some polish. If the store's closed, I'll just rip the door from the hinges with these." She rolled up one sleeve and contracted her biceps. She glanced at Ryne, who was having trouble containing his amusement.

"Nice," Ryne said. "I know a few guys on my team who'd like to have those."

Pointing a finger in Ryne's direction, April warned, "You. Stay out of this."

Ryne held up his hands in a defensive posture. "Oh, a lovers' spat. No problem."

"Darling, you're being unreasonable," Wil said. "It was

just a suggestion. If you're opposed to the desk, we won't get it. But what about some lamps?"

April drew in a calming breath. "Whatever you want."

Wil slapped his palms together. "Good. When?"

"Soon. Wait for me in my office. I'll be there as soon as I can. I have something I need to do first."

"Take your time," Wil replied.

Ryne pushed open the door, more than tempted to let the door go as Wil pushed past him. Instead he gave Tyler a patronizing grin. "Nice meeting you," he called out, his smile fading as soon as Tyler disappeared around a corner. "Doesn't seem like your type," he said, adjusting the gym bags on his shoulder and waving April through the door with one hand.

A puzzled frown puckered April's eyebrows. "And just how would you know what my type is?"

Ryne grinned and seemed to force himself out of thought. "I just thought you'd prefer someone more . . ."

"Macho? A jock maybe?" she finished for him. She couldn't resist the temptation to tease. "Wil doesn't need muscle. He's very interesting."

"What does he do that makes him so interesting besides waterproof a new pair of Docksiders every other week?"

April matched him stride for stride as they walked to the rear elevator. "He's in computer work. He solves problems no one else has been able to solve. He's kind of a mastermind in that area."

"Ah, a computer genius," he repeated, pressing the down button. "Well, Mr. Data needs to work on his handshake."

"I thought you were enjoying that."

"About as much as reaching into a bowl full of jello."

"Do I detect a little arrogance in the tone?" April asked as the elevator arrived.

"I was just commenting."

"Not all women like a man who is just eye candy," she said as they stepped inside and she pushed the "down" button. "I, myself, go for the gray-matter over pecs and butts any day."

It was one of the first times in a week she had seen Ryne's face neither animated nor smiling. It reflected first thought, then amusement followed by a straightforward study of her own face, ending with a glance at her lips.

"You're something, coach," Ryne said as the elevator bumped to a stop and the doors opened. He stepped out and headed to the right. "But I haven't quite figured out what."

Ryne stuffed his gym bag in a locker. April was something all right; something that had gotten under his skin. He could see a potentially dangerous situation developing. He shouldn't be concentrating on anything but his knee and definitely not someone who was his trainer and ultimately would be his judge. But she intrigued him. Intelligent, professional, honest, witty and cute, he'd bet his batting average she matched him in a lot of ways. He slammed the locker shut.

And darn, it looked as though she was spoken for.

April changed into a black sports top and some workout shorts. She frowned, noticing that the bruise on her thigh still hadn't faded and tried to tug the hem of the shorts down to cover it. As she walked into the room, she didn't know why she hadn't told Ryne she was filling in for Jenny and teaching the class.

She fastened the remote unit around her waist and set the microphone on her head. As she fiddled with the sound system, a few people found their spots on the floor. She glanced up and felt a small surge of relief when she noticed Ryne wasn't among them.

Suddenly she straightened and slapped her hands to her waist. This was ridiculous. Why did it matter if Ryne was in her class? With renewed energy she strode to the center of the room and began to step up onto the raised platform when she noticed her sneaker was untied. As she bent down to tie it, in the mirrors lining the exercise room, she saw Ryne come in.

He had changed into shorts and wrapped his knee in an elastic bandage. She watched his leg muscles ripple as he crossed the floor with long, strong strides. Somewhere between his entering the room and finding a place in the class, she forgot to breathe. Still bent over with her hands on her shoelaces, she watched him drop his towel and walk toward her.

He stopped just behind her and crossed his arms over his chest. A broad smile curled his lips. "How did you get that?" he asked.

"Diet and exercise," she replied, straightening with a straight face.

Ryne dropped his arms, closed his eyes and shook his head before bursting out laughing. "The bruise."

She tugged at the hem of her shorts. "Caught the edge of my desk."

"Ah, so that's why the computer nerd wants you to get a new one. The old one is a lethal weapon."

"No," she replied quickly, angling him a clipped look. "He just thinks furniture should make some kind of statement and be an investment."

"So next time you and your boyfriend go antiquing, invite me."

"Why don't you two go? You seemed to have hit it off."

"Yeah, I think we bonded."

"Bonded, huh? I guess you could stretch the meaning of the word."

"Looks like we're taking the same class. Maybe you and I can do some bonding of our own." Ryne looked around the room. "Do you happen to know where the teacher is?"

"You're looking at her," April replied as she stepped up onto the platform.

Ryne felt a wide smile curl his lips. "Ah-huh. Then it looks like I'll be watching that bruise rather carefully for the next hour," he quipped as he went back to his place.

April felt the heat rise in her cheeks. This class was going to be very interesting.

She observed him the whole time using the mirrors. He moved with amazing grace and carefully controlled power, following the moves smoothly and making sure his motion didn't put too much pressure on his knee. An excellent student, he proved to also be a big distraction. More than once she missed the beat and had to ad-lib a move when she saw him wink at her as she watched him.

After class, a bevy of workout-clad women surrounded Ryne. He tried to get to the doorway, but the women moved with him like wind blowing a field of grain. Each one appeared more than willing to hang around after class. She noticed how effortlessly Ryne turned his focus from one to another as each vied for his attention. He was apparently as practiced in the art of flirtation as he was in public relations; his adoring fans seemed to hang on his every word.

A particularly curvy blond pushed her way to the front of the group and grabbed onto Ryne's arm. Clad in a clingy pair of spandex workout shorts and a sports bra, she made no attempt to hide her interest in him. The woman whispered in Ryne's ear and he laughed before picking up his water bottle and heading for the door with her hot on his heels.

April made her way to the front of the small crowd. "Mr. Anderson, can I talk to you for a minute?" she asked. She motioned Ryne to the hall. He nodded to his admirers and followed her.

As April walked with Ryne, she felt his hand on the small of her back. She marveled at the very pleasant sensation. His touch was solid yet gentle, lingering maybe a little too long on the arch of her spine. Was it her imagination or was he intentionally brushing her thigh with his as they walked? The contact made her realize that his muscles were much, much harder than she thought they would be. They felt toned and quite powerful. Realizing she had been assessing Ryne's thighs for something other than a therapeutic reason, she tried to break the contact, but he didn't allow it. He stayed right next to her maintaining the connection.

"Thanks for the save," he said. "I didn't think I was going to be able to make it out alive."

"Do you always attract that much attention wherever you go?"

"Unfortunately, yes. I don't have a whole lot of privacy. But it comes with the status. Just like your Mr. Data must have to make some concessions, too. Don't a whole lot of uptight brainiacs chase after him lusting for the newest version of Fortron-basic-c-plus-something?"

She laughed. "Probably. How does your knee feel?"

Reaching down, he massaged his thigh, drawing her attention back to his body and away from his face. "A little tight, but not too bad."

How she resisted the urge to touch him, she didn't know. "When did Dr. McKee take your therapy up a notch?"

"I told him I needed the cardio. I don't want my fitness level to fall back too much with all the inactivity since the surgery."

"I didn't notice you sucking air during class. You seemed to do just fine."

Ryne's eyes narrowed suspiciously. "So you *were* checking me out in the mirror."

"It's my job."

"Is that the only reason you were leering at my pecs for the entire hour?" He saw her eyes widen and stifled a grin. After a few moments of silence, he asked, "Well is it?"

She scowled. "I wasn't leering at your pecs. I have to make sure you don't hurt yourself."

Ryne whistled and she got the feeling he wasn't particularly impressed with her answer. "Are you sure that's the only reason?" he asked.

"Maybe I like your looks," she shot back without thinking. What in the world made her admit that? "I mean I was impressed with the way you followed the routine. Not bad for the first class."

"Not a problem. I just kept my eye on the bruise and did what it did."

She laughed. "Interesting, although I'm surprised you'd actually admit it."

"I doubt that it would sully my reputation much. I don't care what people think of me. I just want to get better and get out of here."

For a reason she didn't immediately understand, disappointment welled. "Oh." She heard her own hesitation and it totally surprised her. "I want you out of here, too," she said, "and as soon as possible." She bit down on her lip. "For professional reasons, of course."

"Of course."

His tone of voice sounded patronizing to her. "Would there be any other reason?"

Ryne's eyes made a slow tour of her face, lingering the longest on her lips. He leaned back, took a protracted look at her. "I think if I told you there was some chemistry between us, you'd deny it. Wouldn't you?"

His question stunned her. He was direct, there was no denying that. She'd been refusing to admit the spark that seemed to flame each time she saw him. There were other things, too; lingering looks when they met somewhere in the building, the quickening of her heartbeat when she saw him through a window. She had chalked them up to an eagerness for him to succeed at the clinic. But were they really?

"Chemistry?" she repeated. "No, I'd say more like competition."

"No, I think it's attraction," he replied with a slanting grin.

"You seem to profess to know a lot of things, Mr. Anderson."

His eyes suddenly sparked with challenge. "I know one thing for sure. You looked great in that pair of jogging shorts and T-shirt, bare ankled in those sneakers, with your hair, not to mention that strategically placed bruise, bouncing around free all through class."

She angled him a smirk. "When you say something like that I want to jump into sweats and run around the blacktop instead of teaching a class."

"Sounds like a good idea. Let's do it."

April's eyebrows puckered. "Do what?"

"I've been wracking my brain for the last week or so trying to come up with something we can do together. Let's jog."

"Are you serious?"

"Dead serious."

"Have you been cleared to run anywhere but on the treadmills?"

Ryne nodded. "I talked Dr. McKee into letting me do a little running every day. I want to be sure I'm in top shape for spring training."

April didn't respond. The start of spring training was only a few weeks away and she had her doubts about Ryne being ready by then. A critical evaluation for Ryne was coming in a few days and she'd know more then. She felt a little disingenuous for not mentioning it to him, but shook off the sensation.

"So what do you say we run?"

"Can't. I'm meeting Wil right after class," she said.

They walked together to the rear exit on the lower level. "Oh, that's right. You're getting a table or something."

"A lamp," she reminded him.

"Should be a titillating conversation on the way in the car. I suppose you'll spend hours discussing the wonders of silicone chips."

"It can be a very fascinating subject."

He shook his head. "I think you're in some serious need of saving from the perils of sheer boredom. How about I whisk you away for a more interesting evening. Unless you think Mr. Data would get jealous." He stopped walking to chart her expression. "He should just give up and let me win. They say the best man should."

April's jaw dropped. "Let you win? The best man?" She smacked him on the arm. "You arrogant, assuming . . . jock."

He threw back his head and laughed with full amusement. "Can't quite find the right word, huh?"

She stared at him open-mouthed. It was impossible to combat the barrage of reactions he could evoke from her with a simple comment or his rich laugh. Words rolled from his tongue as glibly as quicksilver, sounding like the practiced lines of an actor.

"Well as long as you're dreaming the impossible dream of whisking me anywhere," she said, stopping right before she would have pushed the double doors open, "you'll be pleased to know Wil isn't the jealous type."

"What type is he then?"

She mused on the question. "He's logical and serious. Computer people tend to be that way. He feeds facts into a terminal and comes up with a black-and-white solution. He takes the sensible route to the most plausible conclusion. You and I barely know each other, so logically speaking, there's no reason for him to be jealous."

"He sounds like a pretty dull boyfriend."

"I should resent that," April replied.

"And do you?"

"Yes. Yes, I do." Smugly she grabbed the panic bar and pushed the door open. Once outside, she held the door open and turned to face him. She gave him a coy little pout, knowing she shouldn't. And even as the comment escaped her lips, she knew beyond a shadow of a doubt that what she was about to say would be flirting. "Not because of his 'type,' but because he isn't my boyfriend." Letting go, she watched the door slowly close on his handsome face.

"Wait," Ryne called out as he saw her waggle her fingers in a goodbye gesture. He shoved open the door. "What do you mean he isn't your boyfriend?" He watched her walk away laughing.

He didn't get the chance to go after her as some of the ladies from class surrounded him, blocking any chance at a quick exit. There was no sense even trying to escape them. He was outnumbered four to one.

After stashing her gear in her car, April remembered Wil was waiting for her. Ryne had nearly made her forget that she promised Wil she'd have dinner with him. She got to her floor in time to look out the window next to her office and see four women escorting Ryne to his car.

"That Audi only seats two," she quipped as she watched the women fight for positioning. "You can't all get in there with him." She crossed her arms in front of her and let her mind fill with variations of how he was going to get out of there alive. Her eyes widened when she watched Ryne open the passenger door and let the blond from class slide into the seat.

She started to take a few steps to go down to the parking lot and suddenly stopped. "Wait," she muttered under her breath. "What are you doing? If the man wants to make a fool of himself with a bottled-blond bimbo in almost a blouse, why should I care?"

"Did you say something?"

Wil's voice brought her back to reality. She had almost forgotten about him. She turned toward him and shook her head. "Never mind."

Wil studied her curiously. "Are you all right? You look a bit peaked."

"It's nothing," she said, not being entirely truthful. Ryne Anderson had crept under her skin and wouldn't go away.

## Chapter Three

A few days later Ryne's Audi pulled up to the curb just as April stepped out the front door of the clinic. The top was down and he looked great. His hair had been tussled by the wind, inviting her to smooth it back into place. She couldn't see his eyes underneath the dark aviator-style sunglasses he wore, but she knew he was looking into hers.

"How was your weekend, Coach?" he asked, keeping the car at a slow pace as April walked to her car. "Play any catch with the computer chip at the Vineyard?"

He said it with such an autocratic tone in his voice that she laughed out loud. The question made her picture Wil trying to catch a ground ball the way Ryne would and getting bopped in the nose with it instead. Other pictures came rapid-fire into her mind: Wil trying to hit a fastball, Wil crouching behind home plate. Probably the funniest of all was Wil wearing a baseball cap. The thought of Wil with

35

"hat hair" did it. She stopped walking and had to cover her mouth with one hand.

Ryne stopped the car. He pushed his sunglasses low on his nose with the tip of one finger and looked over the rim. "Did I say something funny?"

April shook her head, her silliness passing. "No, I was picturing Wil Tyler playing for the New York Mets." Drawn to Ryne like metal to magnet, April walked closer to his car.

Ryne shook his head. "Well, I can't picture that."

As he spoke April let her gaze fall to the curve of Ryne's mouth. She suddenly wondered what it would be like to kiss him and became grateful that temptation was held at bay, for now at least, by the silver door of the car that separated them. She had never been drawn like this to a man before. The pull became stronger each minute she spent with him.

She put her hand on the car door, her fingers curling across the window frame. "What are you doing here? I know Dr. McKee is gone for the day. We had a three o'clock meeting that he canceled right before he left."

"I'm taking the long way to the Little League field. Roger and I are holding a baseball clinic. Want to come?"

She straightened. "No, I don't think so."

Ryne got out of the car and walked to the passenger side. He opened the door, urging her inside. "C'mon. We'll get your car later. It'll be fun. Jenny's going to be there."

She looked from Ryne to the car. "I shouldn't," she said, getting in. As the door slammed shut, she wondered what in the world she was doing. She watched Ryne jog around the hood and slip in beside her.

"You'll have to stop at my place so I can change first," she heard herself say. "These shoes and sandlots don't go well together." She kicked off her left shoe and massaged her foot. "Excuse me, but you have no idea how uncomfortable high heels can be." She eased off the other shoe and wiggled her toes.

Ryne grinned. "You mean Miss Fitness has been cramming her feet into stylish shoes instead of sensible ones? Doctor, heal thyself."

She grabbed her right foot with both hands and rubbed it firmly. "I'm a therapist, not a doctor. Besides, sensible shoes don't go with designer suits."

Ryne glanced over at her. "You look like you know what you're doing. Maybe you can give me a rubdown later."

"We have trained professionals at the clinic for that," April said, looking at his handsome profile. Their close proximity in the sports car made her aware of the citrus scent of his aftershave. She wanted to cup his cheek and transfer the scent to her fingertips so she could enjoy it longer. He reached down to turn the key and she found herself following the line of his hand to his broad shoulder. He looked at her and winked. It was like a shot of rejuvenating sun.

As Ryne eased the car away from the curb, she began to think that going to her place wasn't such a good idea after all.

"Come in," April said against her better judgment as she got out of Ryne's car and started up the walk to her townhouse. She waited until Ryne was by her side before opening the door. She snapped on the entry light and they faced a large living room decorated in muted brown tones with touches of mauve. "I'll give you the quick tour." She set her purse down on a table near the door and pointed left. "Kitchen, there. Spare room in the back."

"With a computer, of course."

"Of course. And a deck off the dining room." She caught him eying the staircase to her right. "Two rooms and two baths upstairs." Three steps up, she stopped. "Make yourself at home, I'll just be a second."

Ryne walked to the railing. He watched the slit in the center of the back of her skirt shift as she climbed the stairs. When she turned and moved out of sight, he heard the soft click of her bedroom door shutting and then his own long sigh as he ran a hand through his hair.

He tried to keep his mind off her as he toured her living room and then her kitchen. There were still dishes in the sink. On the table sat a coffee mug full of pencils next to a note that said, "Buy shampoo, that herbal stuff." He grinned and crossed over to the sliding glass door in the dining room. He slid it open and stepped onto a wooden deck. Bracing his hands on the top of the rail, he inhaled deeply and listened to the soft sounds of children playing nearby. He closed his eyes and enjoyed the sound.

April was the kind of woman he'd been looking for. At least he thought so. It was just his luck to find her and discover she was spoken for. But this Tyler person didn't seem like the right kind of man for her. He had silicone chips for brains and didn't appear to complement her personality at all. She had a way about her, a strong sure way when she moved, walked and talked. She exuded the physical with her well-toned body, much like that of an athlete. He could tell by talking to her and being with her that she was also sensitive and caring.

Dangerous thoughts filled his mind and it became suddenly clear to him that she not only held his career in her hands, but was well on her way to holding his heart there too. He straightened, leaned against the railing, his weight on one hip and his hands in the pockets of his jeans. So what did he intend to do about it? He had no answer for the question.

He heard the door slide open and turned to the sound. As April stepped out onto the deck, he let his gaze sweep over her. She was dressed in jeans and a blue T-shirt. She looked great. He guessed she'd look as good in a flour sack.

"Why aren't you and Mr. Data living closer to each other?" he asked when she joined him near the railing. "New England and New Jersey seem a little far apart for a daily commute."

"Is that what you were so deep in thought about?" she asked.

"Basically."

She tugged the T-shirt down at the waist. He didn't move, only watched her shoulders shift and her chest rise in a breath. She caught both elbows on the rail beside him, brushing his arm as she did. At her touch, his mind conjured up a picture of him holding her in his arms.

"Come on," he said, sliding his hand from the curve of her elbow to her wrist before entwining his fingers with hers. "Let's walk." He carefully gauged her response. With her hand loosely in his, it would have been easy for her to pull away. But she didn't.

She turned to meet his eyes and he studied her. He was suddenly surrounded by the light scent of her cologne and a sense of the forbidden. He saw her gaze drop to his mouth before rising back to settle on his eyes. They seemed to be hovering on the brink of something neither felt it wise to begin. But it beckoned with a power almost too compelling to fight.

"Walk where?" she asked.

"Down the stairs. Anywhere. Let's just walk."

"Okay, but watch the steps." Her voice dropped an octave and her gaze went from his knee to the deck stairs. "I don't want you to twist your knee."

Ryne furrowed his eyebrows. "It's only three steps. Being an infielder, I do have a certain amount of coordination." Then he laughed. "I promise I won't sue you if I fall." All the color seemed to drain from April's face with his words. He held her by her upper arms, almost afraid she was going to faint. "What's wrong?" He felt a frown of concern replace the smile on his face. "Are you all right?"

"For a minute I thought about what happened to Rob." She took a deep breath.

"Rob? Who's Rob?" Ryne's brows furrowed.

April let out the breath she was holding and gave him a tight-lipped grin. "My brother."

His gaze analyzed her face and he didn't like the tension he found there. "Did something happen to him here?"

"No, nothing. Don't worry about it," she assured. "He

moved away a while ago, and sometimes I just wish he was closer, that's all."

"Are you sure? You still look a little pale."

"Too much weight training and not enough carbs, I suppose. You wanted to walk, let's walk."

The wooden stairs of the deck were wide and echoed as they descended in slow measured steps. Their sneakers hit the tall grass in unison, and they walked, slowly, toward the wrought-iron bench set near a maple tree in the backyard.

Wait," Ryne said, his hand tightening gently around hers. "Don't sit there. It's probably dirty."

At the change in pressure of his touch, April inhaled sharply and then held her breath. She knew she should stop whatever was going to happen right then but he began to move his thumb in lazy circles on her hand and she didn't want the sensation to end.

"In your opinion, would I be dishonoring the silicone chip if I kissed you?" Ryne asked.

"Wil," she said softly, "his name is Wil." She dropped her head backward and closed her eyes, intending to tell him it wouldn't be a good idea. Instead, she realized it looked more like an invitation and snapped her eyes back open just as Ryne turned her toward him and ran both hands up her arms. She swallowed the words that would have asked him to stay. "The kids are waiting," she said instead.

"I know," he agreed with huskiness in his tone.

"You should get going to the field before it's too late."

"Too late for what?"

*To stop this thing that is building between us*, April thought. *We can't let it happen.* "For the clinic," she heard herself say. He moved his mouth close to hers, so close she could feel his warm breath on her face. She forced herself to concentrate on the tiny mole on his cheek instead of the way he was making her feel. "You can't disappoint the kids." Her voice was strained as she made a conscious effort to subtly widen the gap he had made between them.

"I suppose you're right." He reached up and stroked her cheek with the back of his hand. "But you owe me this kiss and I intend to collect it at the proper time."

She pressed her palms firmly against his chest and pushed away. "Ryne Anderson, you're not playing fair."

"I'm not playing at all. Something special is happening between us. I think it started the first day I saw you."

She reached up and covered his lips with her fingertips. "Don't say anything more. We shouldn't be thinking of anything like this."

He took her hand and freed his lips. He pressed her palm to his chest. He knew she could feel his heart thudding. "Then why are you here alone with me?"

"Don't read anything into . . ."

"You got into my car for the same reason I asked you to do it." His heart was running like a jackhammer. It was so unlike him to not have complete control over a situation.

She jerked her hand free. "You're wrong. I just let a friend drive me home."

He caught her by the shoulders and pulled her to him. "I've never backed away from a challenge, and it appears as though you are going to be my biggest one yet. You better hold on tight if you know what's good for the both of us because I suddenly think the right time to collect that kiss is now."

Ryne covered her mouth with his, trying to drive all sensibility from her mind. The kiss was gentle and unhurried as he slanted his head to fit perfectly with hers. His arm pressed more firmly around her shoulders. His right hand moved through her hair in a caress until he felt her kiss him back and he thought it was about time that she did. He kissed her long and hard until he felt her begin to shift. Only then did he lighten his touch and allow her to move away.

"This is not a good idea," she said, her chest rising and falling in soft gasps.

"I know." Ryne brushed his lips across her cheek and kissed her earlobe.

"We have to stop."

"In a minute," he whispered into her ear. "I like holding you."

His breath sent goosebumps down her spine. Her head felt weightless and her stomach churned. She backed away, denying herself any more of the pleasant sensations.

Ryne touched her elbow to stop her from walking away. "You aren't married to the computer chip yet."

"Wil. His name is Wil," she emphasized again. "Please stop calling him everything else but. I feel guilty enough from not insisting that you stop making fun of him the very first time you did." She shivered and knew it wasn't from the cool spring air but from his warm hands skimming up her arms.

"I'm very attracted to you," Ryne said. "I think you know that."

"It could be just a temporary mood."

Ryne moved his hands to her waist. "I don't think so."

It became apparent to April he wasn't about to give up easily. "You and I are in an awkward situation. I know that. If we met, say at a ball game or at the mall, things may have gone along differently." She made sure she held his eyes with her gaze. He had to understand. "I'm going to be one of your judges, Ryne, a person who gets to help decide if and when you're ready to play ball again. We have to be more careful because of it. We have to see things for what they truly are and not let emotion of any type get in the way. It wouldn't be what's best for either of us."

Ryne paused to consider her words. It could be a very uncomfortable situation. "You're probably right." He took her hands in his and looked her square in the eyes. "We shouldn't interfere with the delicate balance of power as it stands." He stepped back and jammed his hands into his pockets. "So, I don't suppose you'll go to Kevin's baseball clinic field with me."

"It's Kevin's little league team you're giving lessons to?"

He nodded. "Me and Roger. Jenny will be there, too."

"I'd better not."

"Even if I promise to behave and only talk to you about pitching and catching?"

April smiled. "You are talking about baseball now, aren't you?"

"Am I?" He turned his own smile up as far as he could and hoped it would be enough.

She shook her head. "One never knows with you, Mr. Anderson. But I think I'd better stay here." She began walking toward the house and realized he wasn't alongside her. She looked back. He was still near the tree. "You can't teach a clinic from my backyard."

"I want you to come."

"Wil's coming over later. He said he needed to talk to me."

Ryne studied her face for a long moment. "You didn't say anything about Mr. Da . . ."

April pointed her forefinger at him.

"I mean, Tyler coming over here."

"I just remembered."

His three long steps put him right next to her. "I guess that definitely puts a damper on my plans."

"We had no definite plans," she reminded him, striding up the stairs and onto the deck. Pulling open the sliding doors, she motioned for Ryne to walk through them.

At the door he stopped and postured a little bow. "Whatever you say, Miss Stevens. I guess I'll be spending the rest of the night wondering what you and Tyler are doing."

"That will be none of your business."

"I suppose not," he said and extended his hand. "Okay then, take my hand for a minute."

She looked at it suspiciously.

"Why?"

"Humor me."

"Okay, but nothing funny now."

As her hand touched his, he grasped it firmly and pulled her into his arms. He kissed her again, the way he had done before, long and hard, not intending to give her any room to breathe or think.

April felt the kiss explode inside her heart as she clutched his shoulders. She felt one of his arms arc around her waist, the other slipped to support the back of her head as he deepened the kiss. Her knees nearly buckled and her head buzzed with white noise which made her forget everything but the feel of Ryne's lips on hers.

Slowly he pulled away, touching his mouth to hers once more before she saw a smile curl his lips. Her breath caught in her throat as his fingers grazed her jawline before pushing a tendril of hair back around the curve of her ear. He had barely touched her at all, but it affected her as much as if he was kissing her again. She looked into his eyes and saw a yearning that completely mirrored her own.

"There," he said as he released her and turn to leave. "Think about that when the computer chip gets here."

## Chapter Four

Deciding that Ryne's suggestion to run was a good idea, April ran as hard and as fast as she could. She wanted to run him out of her mind, run the taste of his kiss off her lips and the touch of his hand from her skin. She pushed harder, concentrating on her stride and her breathing.

She turned the corner and crossed the blacktop of a deserted parking lot. While crossing the barely visible white-painted parking lanes, she wondered if Ryne felt this exhilarated running the bases at City Stadium. She lightly smacked her forehead to scatter the thought. There he was, inside her head again. As hard as she had run, she had not outrun Ryne Anderson.

Picking up the pace, she began, puffing hard, her breath coming in long, controlled intakes and exhales. In a while the only sounds she could hear were her breathing and the slap of her rubber-soled shoes on the blacktop. But when she turned another corner, other sounds joined her. The click of balls hitting bats and thumps of gloves shagging fly balls permeated the air. She pulled her run into a jog, slowing to a walk. She could hardly believe her eyes. She'd run right to the field on which Ryne was holding his baseball clinic for Kevin's team.

Carefully she stopped far enough away from the activity so that he couldn't spot her. She bent forward at the waist and braced her hands just above her knees. Hanging that way, she tried to catch her breath and clear her mind.

Did she run here on a random course or because she subconsciously knew Ryne would be at the field? Had he wedged himself inside her head so firmly that she was losing control?

Straightening, she hung her hands on her hipbones and leaned backward, stretching her back muscles and trying to find the answers to her questions. When she leveled, she looked ahead and instantly picked out Ryne.

That, she guessed, was answer enough.


"I thought you were going to bring April here," Roger said as the rhythmic click of ball hitting bat echoed in the evening air. "I told Jenny we might all go out after the clinic and get something to eat."

"Two hands," Ryne called out to the dark-haired boy in right field. "Cover the ball after you catch it or it could slip out of your glove for an error."

He turned his attention back to Roger who hit a soft ground ball to the shortstop.

"I almost got her here, but she had a date with the silicone chip she's seeing," he said.

"Funny," Roger said, swinging at the next pitch thrown by the teenaged pitcher and driving it to center. "Jenny didn't say anything about a boyfriend."

"April said something like she wasn't involved with Tyler earlier. I wonder. They seem to be together a lot." Ryne furrowed his brow. "Hum. Looks like I need to clear this up once and for all."

"And how do you propose to do that?"

"Well, my man," Ryne said, arching an arm around Roger's neck and holding up a hand to stop the lesson for a moment. "You've heard of 'Seek and Destroy,' haven't you?"

"Yeah," Roger replied in a tone that was more of a question than an answer.

"Well, tonight it's going to be 'Seek and Find Out What The Heck Is Going On.'"

"Isn't that a bit long for a code name?" Roger asked.

"Not for what I have in mind," Ryne replied, releasing his hold on Roger.

Roger turned his baseball cap around so the brim grazed the back of his neck. He tossed a ball in the air and hit it out to second base. "Gawd, I hope we don't get arrested. Spring training starts in a few weeks and I can't make the team if I'm sharing a cell in Riker's with someone named Bubba."

The doorbell rang. Grabbing the doorknob, April suddenly felt a jagged mass of chaos race through her. She didn't want Wil to be on the other side; she wanted it to be Ryne. Her back stiffened as she yanked open the door.

"Wil." She blew out his name in a long puff of air almost relieved it wasn't Ryne. "Come in."

"Darling, look what I have for you." He carried a style chess table, complete with inlaid top into the room. "It's the perfect living room accent piece.'"

"For your house or mine? You know I don't like chess."

"Remember what you said when we were talking about the lamps?"

"Lamps?" April echoed with a touch of dismay in her voice. "What did I say?"

Wil laughed slightly. "You said you'd come and look at the lamps if we did something together afterward."

He placed the table next to the overstuffed mauve chair in her living room.

"There," he said sweeping his hand over the highly polished table top in triumph. "Something we both can do."

"But Wil, I'm no good at chess."

"I told you I would give you another lesson but it will have to be when I get back."

April covered the table with some magazines. Wil promptly removed them.

"Where are you going?" she asked.

"Austria."

"Austria? For what?"

"Business, darling. I have to leave a bit earlier than expected so I won't be here this weekend."

April tucked her lips against her teeth and clenched her fists.

"Don't tell me you're not going to be here on Friday night. Don't you dare," she growled.

Wil held up both hands to defend himself against the exasperation he saw darting around in April's eyes. "I know I promised to escort you to Dr. McKee's dinner party but this is unavoidable."

"You need to be at this party to help me pitch the New York office. We talked about it and you swore to me no power on earth would keep you from going."

"It isn't exactly a power on earth. It's electronic. I need to be in Vienna by tomorrow."

April spun around and faced the window, forcing him to look at her back.

"What is it now? Did Bill Gates decree that you bring back the latest encryption code technology or something?"

She whirled around to face him again. "The New York office was partly your idea, remember? We agreed that the idea of a satellite office was the next step for the clinic. And I feel that unless I offer Dr. McKee some sort of partnership in it, I may lose him altogether. He's the best in his field. I need him, and his reputation, in order to expand and get the scholarship program going."

"You can handle it, darling. Be charming. Make new friends. Blend in."

April eyed him distastefully. "Blend in? I'll be the only one there without a mate. I'll stick out at dinner like a bride without a groom."

Wil laughed. "Or like a sore thumb."

April's expression immediately tightened.

"I was making a joke. Sore thumb, sore muscles. I thought it would make you feel better. It didn't, did it?"

"No," April answered quickly, studying him with a disturbing thought. What was she doing relying on Wil Tyler to fill her social calendar anyway? They weren't dating, weren't even considering it, but somehow she managed to sound like a spurned lover just thinking about going to the dinner party alone. "It's just that I hate marketing on a social level. That's more your area."

"I know," Wil conceded, "but one of my clients needs some work done quickly. It's sensitive material and he insists I handle it personally. You understand."

April swiped at the air with one hand. "Go. I'll figure something out or I'll go alone."

"I didn't think you'd be this disappointed. It is a pleasant surprise. When I get back, I'll make it up to you. We'll have dinner at that restaurant by the University you like so much." He looked at his watch. "I really have to get going. I still need to pack."

"Sure," April replied. "No problem."

As soon as the door closed behind Wil, her eyes widened at the realization that he thought she was upset because he'd broken their date. It was the last thing she needed him to think.

She and Wil were business partners, nothing more. She needed Wil to help network and make the vital contacts needed for the Clinic to branch out and to help convince Dr. McKee to lead the expansion with her. She hated schmoozing people but it was second nature to Wil.

Now she had no plan *and* no date. Now what was she supposed to do?

Folding her arms across her chest and leaning against the door, she felt faintly ill. Another disturbing thought flashed through her mind. Maybe going to the dinner party with Wil wasn't going to be a date but the last real date she could remember was with the guy her brother paid to take her to the senior prom.

She closed her eyes and sighed. If she wasn't careful, she probably WAS going to end up alone.

"Get down," Ryne shouted, pushing on the top of Roger's head until his forehead touched the dashboard. "Someone's coming."

Roger slouched down in the passenger seat of the old Buick until the sound of footsteps passed. He pulled the dark sunglasses up and peeked out from beneath the frames. "It's just some guy walking his dog. Not one of our suspects."

"Rog, we don't have suspects," Ryne replied, making himself as small as possible for a man his size, and looking out through the arc of the steering wheel. "We know who we're looking for."

"And we don't have to look very far. That's her house right over there," Roger said, pointing to April's place. "So can we cut the cloak and dagger stuff? I feel like one of the Blues Brothers in this getup. All I need is a black brimmed hat and an attitude."

"Quiet. You look great and you already have an attitude. We need to blend into the background so she doesn't see us."

"Anderson, we're sitting in a swanky Princeton neighborhood in a 1985 Buick wearing dark shirts and sunglasses. I don't think we'll blend into much of anything except maybe a police lineup. Where did you get this car anyway? We look like a couple of ex-cons planning a heist."

Ryne straightened and glanced at April's townhouse before turning to Roger. "Borrowed it from a fan."

Roger's eyebrows pulled into a question. "What fan? Not that blond from the cardio class." When Ryne shrugged, Roger knew he was right. "What did you promise her?"

"An autograph," Ryne replied quickly. The smirk on Roger's face told Ryne his friend wasn't buying it. "Well, maybe I did promise to take her to lunch. But that's all."

Roger snickered. "Maybe for starters."

"Stop," Ryne said, leaning forward and peering through the windshield. "I think I see some movement in there."

Roger's gaze followed Ryne's. "I think what you're seeing is curtains caught in a breeze through an open window. Good thing you're not a detective. You stink at this stuff." He settled back in the seat and threw an arm around the headrest. "OK, Colombo. Tell me again why we're here."

Ryne's tension-tight body relaxed and he slouched back. "I need to find out for sure if Tyler is April's boyfriend."

"Wouldn't it be easier just to ask her?"

"I don't want her to get the wrong idea."

"And I suppose when she looks out her front window and sees flashing lights and us getting arrested for peeping, she'll get the right idea."

"We're not going to get arrested. We're just parked."

Roger opened the window and angled his body so he leaned on the door. "You're hooked on the coach, aren't you?"

"No, I'm just trying to save her from a bad decision. Tyler is all wrong for her."

Roger glanced up at April's townhouse. "From what you've told me she seems to be okay with the preppie."

Ryne tossed his head in a sign of pique. "That milk toast computer geek can't keep her warm on a cold night."

"And I suppose you can?"

"Most definitely," Ryne agreed. "That guy up there with her probably doesn't even know how to turn up the thermostat."

"Your sudden concern for April's comfort does my heart good. For a while there I thought you were losing your touch."

"Me? I'm smooth as silk and ready to move right in. I just need an opening."

Roger gestured toward April's front door. "And it looks like you're about to get one. The competition seems to be leaving early. Now what, hotshot?"

"I'm not quite sure."

"You mean you don't have a plan already worked out?" Roger appeared to work at looking stunned.

"Actually, I thought I'd leave that part up to you," Ryne replied with suitable humility. "Your gift for the impulsive is legendary. That's why I keep you around."

Roger grinned in satisfaction. "It's about time you asked my advice." He reached over and slapped a hand to Ryne's shoulder. "Pay attention. I am about to impart the love secrets of the ages. Of course, but then there will be two of us loose in the world. That may not be a very good idea."

"Roger, stop fantasizing about your inflated reputation and help me out here."

"Okay, okay, here's what I want you to do."

Ryne stood on the front porch of April's townhouse and waved Roger away. Turning to the door, he reviewed Roger's instructions in a low whisper.

"Okay. Be smooth, witty, charming," he said. He took a deep breath and raised his shoulders up and down before doing a slow, lazy circle with his head.

"Wait," he said in a moment of insight. "What am I doing taking dating advice from Roger? He can't pick up a paperclip from a desk without help."

He flattened his hands and pressed down against an unseen force. "I can do this. I just need to be myself."

As he knocked on the door, he began to question his intentions. What on earth was he doing? He had no reason to be in the neighborhood and he certainly wasn't about to lie. Maybe he should dump the strategy and come right out and ask April if she was involved with someone. If she said 'yes,' well, the game was over. But if she said 'no' . . .

The sound of his knuckles striking wood as he tapped lightly made him realize there was no turning back now. Butterfly wings banged against every available space in his stomach, the unfamiliar feeling making him uncomfortable.

The iceman was beginning to melt.

## Chapter Five

The knock on April's door at 10 P.M. startled her. She had just changed into her favorite long T-shirt dress. Now who was coming to see her?

She opened the door. "Ryne." His name came out in a whisper mixed with disbelief and delight. He was dressed in a dark shirt and new jeans. When she looked into his eyes, she saw a hesitation of his own.

"Hi," he said in a tone that sounded ill at ease. The sight of April with her hair loose and tumbling down around her shoulders, little if any make-up and surprise in her eyes, made Ryne deep-six his devil-may-care attitude. "I know it's late, but I was hoping to talk to you."

"Sure, come in." She stepped aside to allow him entrance. "What are you doing here at this hour? Your apartment is clear across town." She closed the door and watched him settle into the middle of her living room.

Standing still, he looked around. "Did I tell you how much I like your place?" he said.

"Thanks," April said, moving to a spot just near his shoulder. She smiled. "I feel safe here."

Ryne put his hands in his pockets and studied his shoes. "I could use something safe right now." What was he saying, where was he going with this? He had no idea, only that the words seemed to be coming out of him easily and comfortably. He lifted his head and got lost in her eyes.

"Safe? I don't think I understand."

"The uncertainty surrounding my career has me scattered a little right now. I'm not used to that. I almost feel like I'm a rookie with a cloudy future again."

Sensing his wariness, she reached out and slid her fingers around his arm. "That I understand." She steered him toward the earth-toned sofa. "Sit down. How about some coffee?"

"Sure, sounds good. But make it decaf. Don't need to be up all night." He sat down, hands clasped between his legs.

"I'll be right back," she said, heading for the kitchen.

Watching her leave, Ryne was aware of a heat that settled in his heart. She understood him, understood athletes. He felt it. It was just one more reason to be attracted to her as much as he was. Forcing the feeling aside, he absorbed the peace that surrounded him.

The plants that were in each room gave him a homey feeling. His mother loved plants. They were in every room of the farmhouse, much like they seemed to be everywhere here. There were fresh cut flowers on the table against the wall across from the sofa. Briefly Ryne wondered if Wil had brought them with him when he came to see April, and made a mental note to replace them with something else, something he would choose for her. The room spoke of someone who embraced nature and solitude, just like he did. When he heard the microwave beep and leaned toward the sound he caught sight of pots of herbs on the kitchen windowsill. The house was inviting and feminine, directly opposite to his world of dugouts, wooden benches and locker rooms. He felt comfortable here. Maybe a little too comfortable.

April returned a few minutes later with two mugs on a bamboo tray. "Instant is the best I can do at such short notice."

"Nuked it, huh?"

"I'm not much of a coffee cook, but I can promise you won't glow."

"I'm sure it's fine," he said. He watched her slide the tray onto a table next to the sofa. "Was that here earlier?" he asked.

"Wil brought it with him today."

"I didn't know you played chess." He reached for one of the mugs and analyzed Wil's gift. The sharp lines of the table and the rich inlaid squares didn't appear to fit her decor. He cradled the cup between his hands, thinking he didn't fit in here either.

"I don't. I have to find a place to hide it." Curling up on a chair opposite him, April tucked her legs beneath her and held her cup with one hand. "Now, what's bothering you? Did something happen at the clinic you were holding for the kids?"

"No." He took a large gulp of the coffee. "Thanks for letting me in. I know it's late and we both have a heavy schedule tomorrow."

"I'm not too busy to talk. What's going on? You look lost."

"I guess I am. A little anyway." Ryne's hands tightened around the coffee mug to the point of thinking he might shatter it before he backed off and held it more gently. "This is awkward. In the Bigs, nobody really tells anyone else how they feel." He raised his gaze and held hers. The shadows in the room caressed her cheekbones and emphasized her eyes. He wondered briefly how her long lashes would feel fluttering against his neck and it nearly was his undoing. "The competition learns quickly to use your weaknesses against you."

"Uh-huh. You think coming here to talk is a sign of weakness?" April asked without accusation. She knew being a professional athlete was one of the most competitive jobs ever.

"Maybe weakness isn't the right word, but giving away your emotions gives the other guy the edge."

"And you don't want me to have an edge?"

Ryne blew out a long breath of air. "That's not it."

"Working in rehab, I've come to know first-hand what a high-pressure job being an athlete really is. There's always someone waiting for you to fail so he can take your position."

"Right." Ryne slowly turned the cup around in his hands.

April grew very still as she saw Ryne struggling to speak on what had to be a highly emotional topic for him. Athletes rarely discussed their fears like this. Her brother never had. Rob knew just one thing; play and play hard no matter what. She'd never seen Rob lower his guard like this. Not even when his future was on the line. She wondered why Ryne felt the need to open up to her? They barely knew each other. Whatever the reason, it felt right. She had the wild urge to sit next to him, wrap her arms around his shoulders and hold him. The feeling was warming, but she fought it. "Are you worried that someone is after your job?" she asked gently.

"At this stage of my career, it would be foolish not to think about it. I'm thirty-one, coming off knee surgery and in the option year of my contract. There's always someone younger, faster and better waiting to step in if given the opportunity." His words sounded strained. "And right now I can't play, can I?"

"Ryne, if you've come here to discuss your rehab time-table with me, I can't tell you anything yet."

"I didn't, exactly. I honestly don't know where this is all coming from. I'm not ordinarily this candid." Ryne laughed. "As a rule I try to finesse the answer I want out of the person I want it from."

April didn't laugh with him. "A technique like that usually comes from someone who's . . ." she stumbled over the word. "Scared."

Ryne's head snapped up, a raw nerve suddenly exposed. "I wouldn't use that word."

She looked off into the distance and closed her eyes, her shoulders stiffening.

"If you do know something," Ryne challenged, hearing

the panic in his own voice, "I'd rather not read it in to-morrow's paper."

Slowly her eyes opened. She grimaced and held his gaze. "It's just that right now you remind me so much of my brother. Maybe I'm the one who is scared."

Ryne said nothing. He allowed a moment of quiet to filter between them until her shoulders finally dropped and he sensed she had relaxed a little. "You hardly talk about him. Maybe it's none of my business, but did something happen between you two?"

"We were very close once." A terrible feeling of reliving the past assailed her. "I haven't told many people about what happened."

"Why?" he urged gently.

April stared beyond him to somewhere else in time. Why she was going to tell him, she didn't know. All she knew was that she had to. "My brother, Rob, was a star athlete in high school. He was headed for a full football scholarship at Michigan State."

"Wow, he must have been something on the field. They just don't give those things away to anyone."

"He was."

"Something happened to change that?"

"Rob and I were horsing around one day after football practice in the late fall. You know, brother-sister stuff. We were pushing each other, hitting each other's arms while we said horrible things about each other's anatomy." She bit down on her lip as her throat constricted. "When it was my turn, I pushed Rob and he fell." Her fingers tightened on the coffee mug until her knuckles turned white. "He fell

down the back porch steps and slammed onto the patio."
She felt the sting of tears behind her lids and forced them
back.

Ryne blew out a long breath of air before speaking. "Let
me guess. His knee got messed up."

April nodded. "He begged me not to tell anyone. The
big game with our high school's rival was only two days
away. I helped him ice it and hide the injury from everyone." She blinked her eyes several times as she felt tears
on her lashes. "Well, he played in the game and took a
hard hit from an opposing defenseman." She paused and
pressed her lips together. "They had to carry him off the
field on a stretcher and he never played football again."
She felt the tears begin to trail down her cheeks and was
helpless to stop them. "I should have done something or
told someone."

Reaching over, Ryne placed his hand on her arm. "You
did what you felt was right."

"Maybe I could have said something that would have
changed his mind about playing in the game that night.
Maybe it could have saved his career."

"I doubt it. We athletes can be a very stubborn breed
when it comes to playing."

April was wildly aware of Ryne's hand on her arm. His
touch was electrifying, dredging up more feelings than just
those for her brother and what happened. She wanted to
throw herself into his arms and let him hold her, maybe
stroke her hair, touch her cheek. But she refrained, man-
aging only a weak smile.

Rubbing her brow, she looked at his shoulder so she

wouldn't look into his eyes. "I remember Rob and me having nothing but terrible fights after that. And it wasn't just me. He fought with everyone. Then one day, when I got home from school, Mom called me into the living room and told me that Rob didn't live with us anymore." She shrugged. "I never heard from him again."

Eyes narrowing, Ryne studied April for a long moment, digesting what she had just told him and trying to gauge the impact it had on her life. "Rob dropped all contact with the family because he couldn't play football?"

"Appeared that way. From that day on I swore that I would do whatever I could not to let anyone down again. So I geared the future around sports and ended up here somehow." She laughed. "Sometimes, I don't even remember how." When he smiled back at her, the sight was like a gentle kiss to her bruised heart.

"Criminy," Ryne whispered. "I can't believe he didn't consider what his asking you to help him might cost you."

"It's okay," she reassured with a nervous laugh. "I don't blame anyone but myself. I went along with Rob's decision."

April's brother was an idiot in Ryne's mind and if Rob was here right now, Ryne would tell him so. For now, he remained quiet about it. Rubbing his jaw, he said, "So, indirectly, your brother is responsible for your career."

She nodded. "It all really came together for me during the last two years of college." She hesitated, unsure if she should keep talking about some of her innermost secrets. But the compassion she saw in Ryne's warm brown eyes made her go on. "I changed my major to physical therapy to put to rest the ghosts of the past. After some more schooling and some interning at a few top rehab centers, I opened Princeton Sports Medicine with a mission and with priorities. I do have some accounts to settle first, but I want to make sure that kids never have to make the decision Rob had to make if at all possible. I can make a difference. I know I can. I just wish Rob could be a part of it, too."

Ryne got up, walked to her and held her face between his hands. "Promise me something."

His hands were warm on her skin. His touch was gentle, yet she could feel its strength. "What?"

"When and if you decide to ever try to find your brother, take me with you. Maybe I can help. I mean, I know the type. Intimately."

She searched Ryne's somber-looking features and knew he was serious. "I tried a few times, but I don't think Rob wants me to find him."

"Just know the offer will always be there for you."

With a nervous laugh, April shook her head and Ryne moved his hands away from her cheeks. She had said too much, let him too far inside. "If and when I ever do, I'll let you know. Unless, of course, you're living in a mansion in Hollywood with a wife and seven kids. Okay?"

"Sure," Ryne said with a slanted smile. "But six kids, and I still go with you."

"Deal." Briefly she felt that he might be the one to help her salvage the tattered bits of her soul. Single-handedly she had been trying to hold her spirit together, never letting anyone get too close. It was a hard, lonely struggle and often she dreamed about someone to help her finally succeed. Over the last few weeks more than once, she thought that person might be Ryne.

She wanted to trust him with this part of herself, but how could she? When she really thought about it, the stakes seemed too high for her to ignore. Ryne was an athlete, and could very well end up just like her brother. That would be the definitive, devastating blow. She couldn't go through that again.

Panic made her retreat. "I'm sorry. I'm not even sure why all that came out, but once I started talking about Rob, I couldn't seem to stop."

"You're something else," Ryne said, pulling her to standing and not letting go of her hands.

"Really? What am I?"

"Something completely different from what I expected in a physical therapist, slash, business owner. You're actually in this business for something other than fortune and glory."

"Fortune and glory," she repeated. "You mean like athletes?"

"Some maybe."

April relaxed a little with the change in tone. "But, of course, I didn't mean you."

"Of course." His gaze held hers. "Sometime I'd like to hear more about your brother."

"It's a long, complicated story, Ryne. I don't think you really want to hear the rest."

"Yes, I do." His voice was husky with emotion. "I can understand how your brother felt. Maybe I can help you understand it, too."

An explosion of dismay ripped through April. How easy it would be to fall under the spell of Ryne's incredible eyes and get lost in the comfort he was offering her now. How easy it would be to lean over right now and kiss him.

She pulled her hands free. "It still scares me sometimes."

"I didn't come over here tonight to do that to you."

"You never did tell me why you came."

"I started out to do some investigative research," Ryne admitted. "But it seems like in the process, I've stirred up some memories I should have let stay in the past where they belong. I feel terrible about that. Is there anything I can do to make up for what I put you through?"

"Actually," April tapped her chin thoughtfully, the tension flowing out of her body as the solution to one of her more immediate problems surprisingly presented itself. "There is one thing."

"Name it, it's yours."

"I need a date."

"A date?"

April saw the intensity in his eyes change. "Yes. Aaron McKee is having a dinner party tomorrow night. I hate to go to things like that alone."

"What about Chip?"

"Chip?"

"Chip Nerdgeekson, the computer wizard." April raised her finger in a warning gesture. "I mean Tyler," he continued. "Why would he let you go there alone?" His mind was already spinning with the opportunity that had just been laid in his lap.

"Business trip. He said it was unavoidable."

"Lucky for me."

"Then you'll go?"

"Just tell me when to pick you up."

"Eight o'clock. Here."

"It's a date." He patted her hand. "Listen, I'd better go. It's getting late and we both need some sleep. I have that stress test on my knee tomorrow."

She had almost forgotten about that test. She'd know more about how his knee was coming along when she saw the results. Then there was the meeting with Rockets' management the next day. Everything was happening so fast.

She stood and took the cups to the kitchen. Ryne followed her. When she turned around, a foot separating them, she heard him speak in a low tone.

"April, I didn't mean for it to get so personal."

Looking at the pleasing curve of his lips, she swallowed hard. "I know." A soft sound came from her throat when she felt his arms go around her.

Automatically her eyes locked with his. He drew her closer, the moment fragile as she knew one word from her would break the enchantment. His breath caressed her cheek as his lips came closer to hers. When they touched hers, she surrendered to his arms.

Sensations assailed her. The scrape of a beginning beard against her skin, the brush of his lips on hers all sent a delicious prickle through her. His kiss was soft, questioning, but she felt inherent strength along with incredible gentleness as his mouth molded to hers.

Sliding her arms around his neck, she stretched upward and savored the moment. She caught the masculine scent of his aftershave and threaded her fingers in his dark hair. She didn't want the kiss to end but gradually he broke contact with her, their breaths mingling. They stood looking deep into each other's eyes until he pulled her to him and settled her into the curves of his muscular body.

"I've been wondering when I would get to kiss you again," Ryne admitted in an uneven voice. "Now that I have, I'm wondering if it's going to change anything between us."

Heart pounding erratically in her chest, April lifted her chin and was lost again in the deep brown of his eyes. The words wouldn't come and she saw him give her a smile filled with tenderness. He stroked her hair and placed a kiss on her cheek.

"I don't expect you to tell me now," he said, memorizing how she looked in the soft light.

"Good, because I don't think I can," she replied.

Reluctantly Ryne freed her and took a step backward. "Fair enough." He smiled fully. "At least we do have a date."

"I suppose we do."

Ryne winked. "Good night then." He left quietly without looking back.

She just stood there looking at the door as it slowly closed. What on earth had she just done?

## Chapter Six

April awakened with a serious headache. *The meeting with Dr. McKee*, she thought. *I don't want to have it after last night.* She curled into a small ball and shut her eyes, reliving Ryne's kiss and realizing they'd be spending the evening together.

She considered calling Jenny and telling her what she had done, but decided against it. If past practice became future ritual, Jenny would tell her to go for it. But she couldn't go for anything, least of all Ryne Anderson, even if she wanted to. She had a job to do and emotion simply had no part in it.

She dressed in a navy suit with a simple white blouse. Her hair hung loose and uncurled. Fluffed only by a blow dryer, it was totally natural. She avoided all make-up except some mascara. As she applied some light-colored gloss on her lips, she decided that she and Ryne had done too much "going for it" lately. She grabbed her purse and headed for the door. It was definitely going to stop, no matter how pleasant it had been.

She was running about fifteen minutes late and fully expected to see Ryne as she parked the car in the lot at the Clinic. To her relief, he wasn't anywhere to be seen. But Dr. McKee's car was in his usual spot, turning that relief into a tiny point of panic. She couldn't seem to concentrate on her clinical side when the emotional one was rampaging through her mind.

She had just locked the car when she saw Ryne's car pull into the parking lot. Her heart went into overdrive. She watched him slip the car into an empty spot and get out. Even with the dark glasses hiding his eyes, she thought he saw her.

She started to wave, but he walked to the passenger side of his car and opened it. Out stepped a pretty blond. April recognized her as one of the women from the aerobics class.

The two of them walked toward the building and April followed, wondering why she felt such a deep sense of abandonment while looking at Ryne's back as he walked with another woman. She heard the woman laugh and her heart sank.

They stopped at the door and just as Ryne's hand rested on the bar, he looked back over his shoulder. When his gaze locked with hers, April turned and started walking back to her car.

"Wait," he called out, hooking his sunglasses on his shirt by the earpiece. "April, wait."

She stopped short, her mind filling with hope but she had no idea why.

"I accidentally took something of yours home with me last night," he said when he reached her.

She turned to face him and saw him dig into his right pants pocket. When he pulled out his hand, a hoop earring was looped around his finger. He held it out to her as she walked toward him.

As she got closer to him, the wonderful aroma of the same cologne he wore last night when he was with her brought back some wonderful memories. She smiled, pleasant feelings warming her until she saw the blond over his shoulder still waiting by the door.

"One's not much good, is it?" he asked.

"No, I suppose not," she said. "Thank you."

"I don't even know how it got tangled in my clothes, but I found it in my shirt pocket when I got home last night."

Next to him now, she held out her hand and he dropped the earring into her palm. "I didn't notice it was missing." She glanced over his shoulder at the blond and quickly looked away. Ryne started to walk back to the building, but April hesitated.

"Aren't you coming in?" he asked, a puzzled look crossing his face when turned back and watched April spin on her heels.

"No, I have to go," she stammered, striding away. She stopped at her car door and looked back. Ryne stood unmoving, the bewildered look still on his face.

And that's exactly where he stayed when April got in

the car, slammed her car door, spun her tires and roared out of the parking lot.

Now she was thirty minutes late.

"Don't you dare say a word." April pointed a warning finger at Jenny as she strode past on her way to her office. "I know I've kept Aaron waiting."

"He's not in there." Jenny said, shuffling some papers on the desktop.

April stopped dead in her tracks. "What do you mean he's not in there?"

"Dr. McKee left about ten minutes ago. He said he had a patient coming in and would catch up with you at the dinner party tonight."

"He can't do that." April walked in her office and walked right back out. "I can't talk to him at the party. Ryne will be there."

Jenny looked totally lost. "Ryne's going to the dinner party? With who? Not that bottle-blond aerobicky thing that comes to all my kickboxing classes? I saw them walk in together about a half-hour ago." She slid her elbows onto the desk and dropped her chin into her hands. "He sure moves fast. He hasn't been here that long and he's already getting busy."

April paced the outer office. "No, he's not going with her, he's going with me. At least I think that he is." She slapped a hand to her head. "What have I done? I don't dare talk to Aaron about Ryne's future with Ryne at my side. I'm almost sure that was what Ryne wanted to talk to me about last night when he was over. But we got distracted and didn't get to the subject. Thank heavens I dodged that bullet."

Jenny stood straight up. "Wait a minute." She walked over to April, grabbed her shoulders and practically dragged her to the nearest chair. "Ryne was at your place last night AND you're going to Dr. McKee's dinner party with him tonight."

"Yes."

"He is certainly getting busy in a short amount of time."

April shrugged. "One minute Wil was going, the next, he wasn't. Then Ryne showed up at my door and the next thing I knew, I asked him to be my date." She grabbed her head with both hands. "My date! What was I thinking? I can't go out with Ryne. He's a client. A very important one at that." A picture of Ryne and the blond in the parking flashed through her mind. "Besides, he's obviously interested in someone else." She grabbed the phone. "I have to cancel."

Pressing a finger to the receiver, Jenny stopped April. "Cancel what? The meeting? The date? The future? Let's think about this for a minute."

Slowly dropping the phone back into the cradle, April nodded. "Yes. Thinking would be a nice change from what I've apparently been doing lately."

"Okay, problem number one, Dr. McKee and his report on Ryne's progress." Jenny pressed on April's shoulders and made her sit. "You need to avoid talking to him about it until tomorrow so you can look Ryne in the eye tonight and honestly tell him you don't know anything."

"How am I going to do that when I have already committed to being at the dinner party with both of them later?"

Jenny cautioned April with her finger. "One dilemma at

a time. I know Dr. McKee is here all day with a full schedule, so you need to leave." She pulled April to standing.

"Now?"

"Right now."

April broke loose of Jenny's grasp and sat back down in the chair. "I can't do that. I'm doing an exit interview with Kevin and his parents in an hour."

"Then you'll leave after that."

"Maybe."

"Okay, then Plan B."

"I didn't know we had a Plan A."

Jenny ignored her. "I'll call Dr. McKee, apologize for your being late this morning. I'll make something plausible up, but you'll owe me." She pointed at April who nodded back. "Then I'll get him to reschedule for a few days from now."

"And what will that accomplish? I'll still see him tonight at the party."

"If he tries to talk to you about Ryne, you simply say that you need your notes." Jenny raised her eyebrows in triumph. "Huh? Is that brilliant?"

April sighed and dropped her shoulders. She closed her eyes and shook her head. "Jen, Dr. McKee is the one with the notes."

"Oh. Right. Well," she waved off the problem with a swipe of her hand. "I'll think of something else to tell him before tonight. Which brings us to problem two. You can't have a date with Ryne."

"I know that, Jen."

"Where's Wil?"

"In Austria."

Jenny scratched her chin with a forefinger. "What is he doing in Austria?"

"Saving the free world for Bill Gates, I imagine."

"So I guess Ryne has to go with you then."

"Looks that way."

Jenny slapped a hand to her hip and began to walk. "So then what we need is to make sure that Ryne knows this arrangement tonight is nothing more than business." She spun and pointed at April. "Of course, he might already assume it's only business and if we say anything to the contrary, then he could suspect that you thought it was a real date, which would make the situation even more awkward than it is." She made small circles in the air with the index finger of her right hand. "Or he could get the wrong idea and think that you want it to be a real date. Or . . ."

"Enough," April shouted, covering her ears. "You're giving me a headache. Just cut to the solution."

"I'm thinking. I'm thinking."

As April watched Jenny continue to pace, she wondered about the countless complications that having a real date with Ryne would bring.

She had no right to even think about starting a relationship with him. Except for what she read in the papers and on her charts, she really knew very little about him. Still, in the few moments they shared over the past weeks, she couldn't help but notice that the impressions she had about him had been pleasant ones. If he wasn't considered her prize venture and she wasn't going to be the one who might end his career before it was time, she very well might be trying to find ways to make sure the evening was more than just a friendly fill-in.

"I know," she heard Jenny say, the excited voice drawing April out of her musings. "Roger and I will go with you to the dinner party and make sure that neither you and Ryne nor you and Dr. McKee are ever alone together."

April looked at Jenny and sighed. "I haven't been chaperoned since high school."

"Take it or leave it," Jenny replied. "It's all I have."

As far as plans went, it wasn't a very good one. "I'll take it," she heard herself say. "And let's just hope Aaron's house is big enough for us all."

Inside City Stadium, just above the second level in left field in the executive office suite, a distinguished older gentleman stood in front of the floor-to-ceiling window that overlooked the impeccably trimmed infield. Hands clasped behind his back, he rocked back and forth on his heels as he watched a few of the groundskeepers work on an area near home plate.

"Spring training will be here before you know it, Tommy," he said, watching another of the grounds crew rake the infield dirt. "Can you believe another season is starting already? It seems like just yesterday we won the series."

Tommy Williams, former nine-time All-Star for the New York City Rockets and, at 45, the youngest coach the organization ever hired, walked over to a nearby chair and lowered himself into it. "Sit down, Dick, you look as jumpy as a rookie pitcher with the winning run on third."

Dick Erhart, Rockets' owner and general manager, turned slowly. He walked to the chair behind the cherry wood desk in the middle of the office suite and, after running his hand over the deep brown leather and staring at the framed team photo on the wall, sat down. "Do I have a reason to be jumpy, Tommy?"

Williams shrugged. "Not yet. In a few weeks, pitchers and catchers report to Tampa for spring training and Roger Taylor's ready. Just finished reading the report from the rehab clinic and our team doctor. He's been cleared to play."

"I'm not worried about Taylor. The rest of the team is supposed to check in a week later. What do you hear on Anderson? We need him back at the hot spot if we want to repeat the championship in October."

"I know that." Williams got up and walked to the window. He pointed in the direction of third base. "Remember the sixth game of the World Series? If Anderson hadn't caught that screaming liner, we wouldn't be talking about repeating anything."

"You didn't answer the question."

Williams spun around and crossed his arms in front of his chest. "I know that. Dr. McKee has put off our meeting. He said he needs more time to evaluate Anderson's knee."

"How much time?"

He took off his baseball cap emblazoned with the Rockets' logo and scratched his head. "Another couple of weeks."

"And you think we can start pre-season without a solid third baseman."

Williams ran a hand through his hair and replaced the cap. "I think we owe it to Anderson not to fill his spot on day one."

Erhart joined Williams at the window. He gestured to the centerfield fence. "How many dingers you think Anderson dumped over that thing?"

"Total?"

"In all his time with us."

"I don't know."

"Guess."

"Three hundred?"

Erhart slapped his coach on the back. "Not even close. Four hundred ninety-seven. Pretty darn good."

"I sense a 'but' here."

"That's why I hired you, Tommy. You know things." Erhart gestured to the other side of the room with a nod of his head. Neither said a word as they walked to the custom-built oak bar lining the rear wall. "What'll you have?"

"I think I'm going to need something stronger after we finish talking, but I'll take a seltzer for now."

Erhart tossed a coaster on the highly polished counter, twisted the top from the bottle he had retrieved from the refrigerator underneath the bar and slid it toward Tommy. "You know as well as I do that at our level, baseball is not just a sport. It's a business."

Not bothering with a glass, Tommy took a long swig from the bottle, wishing it had more kick than just some carbon dioxide bubbles. "Only to the accountants, Dick."

"Still, as a businessman, I need to make a business decision." Erhart leaned down and pulled out some papers from the dark leather briefcase he had stashed on the floor behind the bar. He handed them to Williams. "We signed a free agent today."

"Who?"

"Herb Cabot. He's going to help us out at third."

"Geez, Dick," Tommy said taking the papers in disbelief. "I heard he was going to sign back with the Dodgers."

"He was. Until we threw some numbers at him."

"Isn't this a bit premature?"

"I can't take a chance of Anderson not being ready in time and then having to start some rookie from triple-A ball at his spot."

Tommy slid the papers back in Erhart's direction. "When the media gets hold of this, they're going to make mincemeat out of Anderson and draw all sorts of conclusions about his knee."

"It's nothing personal."

"Can't we have waited a little while? At least until we heard from the doctor. He could clear Anderson to play in a week. Two at the most."

Erhart shook his head. "I have a gut feeling about this. Cabot's ready now, and he might not be available in a few weeks. I have to think of the team's future."

As Tommy Williams took another healthy drink of his seltzer, he couldn't help but wonder who was going to think of Ryne's.

## Chapter Seven

"**S**tandard Pizza. You call it in, we haul it out." Roger covered the receiver with his hand. "I love keeping people off-balance." He turned his attention back to the caller and laughed. "No, you have the right number. He's here. Who's calling?" He cradled the phone into his shoulder. "Hey Anderson, your lady's on the phone."

Lifting his head from the paper he was reading, Ryne saw Roger grinning from ear to ear. "What did you say?"

"April Stevens is on the line. Don't you want to talk to her? She wants to talk to you."

Ryne looked at his watch. He had a few hours until he was supposed to pick April up for the dinner party. He hoped she wasn't calling to cancel. He got up and nearly ran to the phone. "Thanks, now go away," he said, jerking it from Roger's hand.

"What if I promise to plug up my ears? Can I stay?"

"Hold on a minute, April," Ryne said into the receiver before holding the phone to his chest. "No. Eavesdrop from another room."

"Like you could stop me anyway," Roger mumbled, heading for the kitchen.

"Hey," Ryne said into the receiver. "This is a nice surprise."

"I'm sorry to bother you at home," April said from the other side of the line.

"No, that's okay. You don't sound good. Anything wrong?"

"Could I pick you up tonight instead of you coming to get me?"

Ryne felt his face tighten in a scowl. "Sure. If that's what you want to do. I understand Roger and Jenny will be at the dinner party. I thought we were all going together." His mind whirled with reasons April might be changing the plan.

"No. I don't think I can take a start-to-finish evening with the King of Comedy," April said. "I'll be there at seven."

"Seven it is. I'll be ready and I'll be Rogerless," Ryne said.

He hung up the phone, not liking the tone he heard in April's voice. She sounded upset. He wondered why and it must have shown on his face.

"You look like you have a perplexity running around in your head," Roger noted when he came back into the room.

With a snort, Ryne walked toward his bedroom. "Sounds about right."

Roger nodded toward the phone. "The lady with the deep, rich voice has you tied up in knots, does she? I've never seen you this strung out before. Not even when we were almost eliminated by the Mets last year."

Ryne stopped at the door and turned back to Roger. "In that game, at least I have some control over what I can do to help the team." He rubbed his chin. "I'm not sure I even know what team I'm on with April."

"You're really serious about this lady, aren't you?"

"I'm not going to lie to you, Rog. I wake up thinking about her and I go to sleep and dream about her."

Roger smiled. "Looks good on you."

"What does?"

"Buddy, I think you're in love."

April had a white carnation in her hand when Ryne answered the doorbell. "For me?" he asked as he took the flower when it was offered. His gaze slid up her frame from the simple black dress she wore to the small diamond earrings that seemed to bring out the light in her eyes. "Come in."

"I thought I needed to bring something. I don't know why." April absorbed his features, smiling as her gaze assimilated each one.

"That's cute." He walked into the kitchen and grabbed a tall glass from the cabinet. "But we're not going to the prom or anything," he said, setting the flower inside and filling the glass. He slid it onto the windowsill above the sink. "I'm your second choice for this date, remember?"

"Don't take it so hard."

"I'm not," he lied. "It won't be so bad. It gives me a chance to dress up, show off my hunky body in a suit instead of sweats and, heck, I'm not that bad of a dancer if need be."

"Hunky body, huh?" April laughed. She actually loved his teasing. "And I don't think we'll be doing much dancing. This party is not pleasure."

"I know. But we don't have to get caught up in business all night, do we?" He motioned to the sofa and she sat down.

"For most of it, I hope. I really want to open up that branch office in New York City and get Dr. McKee to agree to head it. This networking opportunity with a few of the top orthopedic surgeons in the region is very important."

"I'll try to be the perfect window dressing then."

"You don't have to go," she said suddenly. "If it makes you uncomfortable."

"I want to go," he said with a grin.

April matched his smile. "Good, because I'm really going to need your help. I'm not very good at schmoozing." She looked at him and narrowed her eyes.

"Hey, I can be the King of Schmooze." He glanced at his watch. "We'll have plenty of time to talk about what you want me to do and when. You're really early. You'll have to entertain yourself while I get ready."

"Is Roger here? I can talk to him."

"No. He left to pick up Jenny."

"So we're alone then?"

He walked over to where she sat. "Does that bother you?"

She sensed he was testing her and stood. They were inches from each other. "No. Should I be?"

"You're not afraid I might ask you for a real date?"

She gave him a narrowed look. "I'd have to turn you down if you did."

Ryne reached out and touched her hair with the back of his hand. The silky curls sent intoxicating images through his mind. He leaned down until his lips were only a breath away from hers. "Then I'd have to keep asking you until you said yes."

"That could take a very long time," she said in a voice that was more a whisper.

He threw his head back and groaned eloquently. "I'm normally not a very patient man."

"Then it would be a new experience for you."

"I suppose it would." Ryne remained silent for a minute. When April took a small step backward, he felt a smile slant across his mouth. With a chuckle he gestured toward the back of the house. "Why don't you snoop for a while and I'll get ready."

April shook her head. "You're just full of surprises, aren't you?"

"Is that macho athlete image staring to fade from me yet?" he teased.

April blushed. "Maybe a little bit."

Ryne laughed. He turned and walked down the beige-carpeted hallway. "Make yourself at home and see what you can find out about me in fifteen minutes while I get ready for our non-date."

She watched him disappear into a back room. He said she should snoop, so snoop she would.

Over the years she had learned to tell a lot about people just by the feeling she got from the things that surrounded them. She stood quietly and sensed a liveliness filtering though her. Ryne's home, temporary as it was, seemed spirited, but not overly stimulated.

The room in which she stood was an active mixture of colors and textures. The walls were pale yellow and the rug the same tan that lined the hallway. To one side, an overstuffed plaid sofa and chair faced a big-screen TV set, obviously for watching the ball games. The other side of the room served as a formal dining room with a Victorian-style table with shaped feet surrounded by Windsor chairs. Although the oval walnut tabletop seemed to show an attempt at some type of care, a few water rings marred the surface. She ran her hands over the satin finish and guessed a good rubbing would save it from total destruction.

Beyond the large room in which she stood, the kitchen was bright and airy, modern with all the trimmings. A wooden breakfast group sat in the sunniest corner overlooking the back yard. What made her smile the most were the pots of herbs lining the windowsill behind the sink where Ryne had put the carnation. She had many of the same growing on the ledge in her own. She leaned over, inhaling the scent of sage and spearmint. Did Ryne cook, or did Roger, she wondered.

Next to the kitchen, she discovered a small office. There was not much room for more than a desk and a bookcase. She shifted through the newspaper clippings spread next to the computer and found that most of them were on Ryne and his rehabilitation. She saw him grin up at her from an old cover of *Sports Illustrated* and laughed out loud when she saw the glasses and moustache someone had penciled over his face on the cover of *GQ*. Roger, she guessed, had done that deed.

She noticed several photos that hung on the wall and was surprised to find they were all family pictures. One was obviously with Ryne's parents, others of him were with what could only be brothers and sisters. Five siblings in all. Curious, she studied the family.

Ryne's mother was small, with graying hair in a bun atop her head and a warming, welcoming smile. His dad was tall and powerfully built. A handsome man, he was wearing coveralls. The picture was apparently taken quickly, without giving them much time to prep. Still, in it she saw warmth and friendliness. She liked that.

Ryne seemed to have more of his mother's features, she concluded, looking closer at the two of them together. His smile was much like hers and he definitely had her eyes. The firm edges of his father's jaw line underscored Ryne's face. For some reason, she liked that too.

The photo farthest on the wall was that of a much younger Ryne shaking hands with a distinguished-looking man. She guessed Ryne must have been just out of high school then or in his early college years. His faced looked relaxed, unlined, untouched by life as yet. She made a mental note to ask him about it.

The door beyond the last picture was ajar and she walked through it.

One step inside the next room and she jerked to a stop. She had walked into Ryne's bedroom and he was in the process of pulling a crisp, blue shirt across his shoulders. Surprised, she took a quick step backward.

"Don't go," Ryne said, quickly doing up the buttons on the shirt. "I'll be decent in a second."

April couldn't seem to tear her gaze from him. The strong lines of his upper body moved with a grace she didn't expect from a man.

"Like what you see?" he asked playfully.

April was suddenly grateful the continued verbal sparring she used to do with her brother when they were younger had developed a finely honed drollness she still could use. "Coming from some other guy, that would be a line, but I suspect you mean the room."

Ryne laughed with her. "Yes, it would. But I am an honorable man." He pulled out a jacket from the walk-in closet. "Check out the antique bed. Roger said he bought it at an auction at Sotheby's."

"You're kidding," April said as she walked toward it. "It's beautiful." She ran her hand over the smooth, cold bars that made up the footboard. "How old do you think it is?"

"A couple hundred years, I think. At least that's what Roger told me the auctioneer said."

Ryne joined her near the footboard, hands on hips, coat casually draped in the arch formed near his waist on his right. "Want to sit on it?"

April stepped away, finding his easy manner too irresistible. "At least you didn't ask if I wanted to see your etchings." His hair was still slightly damp from the shower and he had opted not to shave, giving him a slight five-o'clock shadow and making him look dangerous to her. The situation would have even seemed more precarious if she cared to acknowledge the rise in her heartbeat or the fact that she felt light-headed being alone with him.

"No," he protested. "I just thought you'd like to close your eyes and pretend to be part of a time when things were less hectic and much simpler. The eighteen-hundreds, I believe."

As she centered herself, April raised her eyebrows. "Roger never ceases to amaze me. Who would have guessed he had an interest in antiques."

"Hey," Ryne said, not even trying to hide his amusement. "Maybe he and your boyfriend can check out the bargains at the historic shops on the Cape someday. That'll free you up to have some real fun." *With me,* he added silently as he saw April roll her eyes and quickly leave the room the same way she came in.

## Chapter Eight

"How did you like the family pictures?" Ryne asked, looking both ways before pulling his Audi out into traffic. He resisted the urge to shoot into the left lane to pass the slower-moving traffic and instead cruised along with it. Maybe he was being selfish, but he wanted to spend as much time as he could alone with April before they had to mingle with others at the dinner party.

"Honestly? They surprised me," April answered.

"Why?"

"Well," she hedged, "you're only here for a few months' rehab and I wouldn't expect a sports star to have family photos hanging around his computer."

Giving her a grin, Ryne said in a conspiratorial tone, "You were expecting centerfolds and supermodels?"

She nodded. "I think I was."

"But," he teased, watching her cringe.

Shifting in the seat April muttered, "But you're beginning to mystify me. I assumed all sports heroes dated actresses or incredibly beautiful women." She glanced over quickly to see his reaction.

"Some might, but I date women who interest me."

"Oh, like Malibu Barbie?" April asked impulsively.

"Who?" The word came out in a laugh.

"Malibu Barbie. The blond you were with in the parking lot outside the clinic."

"You mean Candy?

April rolled her eyes. "Candy, huh? That figures."

Ryne laughed heartily. "You sound jealous."

"I do not. I just didn't think you'd be interested in a girl like that."

"Like what," he baited.

"Like Pamela Anderson-Lee. Beautiful, blond, built. Hardly the athletic type that I figured you would be drawn to."

He snickered. "Well, Candy is certainly beautiful, but I'm not interested in her. I owed her a favor."

April eyed him skeptically.

"She let me borrow her car."

Disbelief deepened the frown line across April's forehead.

"Okay, that's too long a story for me to get into right now," Ryne continued, "but I don't just date a woman because she is model perfect."

"So you admit Candy is a model."

Ryne shook his head in surrender. "Okay, she does some print work, but I'm not interested in her, honest."

"Cross your heart?"

He made the sign on the pocket of his shirt. "Definitely."

"I guess I believe you."

"A woman's looks aren't that high up on my list of 'must-haves.' I appreciate intelligence and dedication in a woman. I understand that success comes from commitment and hard work, and I think that over the long term, I'd like the woman I'm going to spend my life with to understand that, too."

April dropped her arms, softening her body language. She looked back into his eyes. "Coming from a farming family, I guess you know all about hard work and commitment."

He nodded. "Those pictures on the wall back at the house tell you who I am and how I got where I am. The farm has been in the family for a hundred years. I'm proud of my parents. They worked just as hard as I did to get me to the majors. I owe them something that's hard to repay."

April felt good about that. Ryne apparently hadn't had anything handed to him on a silver platter. He worked hard and grabbed at his dream. It said a lot about his beliefs and his goals.

"Did you work on the farm?" she asked.

"Since I was about nine. We didn't have much extra money to hire help. When I wasn't practicing or playing ball, I worked on the farm until I graduated from high school."

"You look a lot like your mother."

"Everyone tells me that."

April studied his strong profile as he drove, noticing the

smile lines at the corner of his eyes and the gentle curve of his mouth. She wondered if he was remembering some heartfelt moments with his mother as his lips pulled into a smile.

"And you don't mind," she added.

"Not at all. Mom was a dreamer. She came from a long line of sturdy farm people in the Midwest, but she always dreamed about living in New York."

"I think she gave you a little of her dream," April said.

"She did. When I was old enough to throw a ball, she took me to see my first professional ballgame in Chicago. It was a big trip for us. After that I told everyone who would listen that I was going to play baseball someday. She told me I could do anything if I set my mind to it. When I was about twelve, and our little league team won the championship, she told everyone that I was going to New York to play ball some day. She was sure of it."

April felt her heart expand until it seemed as wide as his smile. "You're lucky to have someone that supportive."

"It wasn't all play and no work. Dad made sure that the farm chores were done before anything. I remember one time, on a day when the herd didn't want to cooperate, it got dark before I had time to practice. Mom pulled the tractor up to the field and turned on the headlights so she and I could shag a few fly balls."

"I bet that was a sight."

"It was right up until the minute Dad came out of the house and realized what we were doing. The game came to a roaring halt when he turned off the engine and the lights went out. Man, he was hot."

Laughed escaped from April and, without thinking, she reached over and placed her hand on top of Ryne's just as he shifted into another gear. She watched him smile at her touch and he shifted his gaze to hers.

"You want to hold hands?" he asked.

She saw hope flare in the dark blue depths of his eyes before he turned his gaze back to the road ahead. "Do you think it would be safe?"

April gave Ryne his answer by not moving her hand from atop his. As Ryne downshifted, preparing to stop at the changing light in front of them, he hooked his thumb over her pinky finger, not preventing her from removing her hand, rather urging her not to do so.

It seemed impossible for her to recover from his innocent, spontaneous gesture. She tried to stop staring at his profile. The soft shadows seemed to accent his mouth. She recalled its strength and its gentleness, and suddenly wanted him to pull over and kiss her. Maybe keep kissing her forever.

Trying to rally from the sensation of sweet fire crackling up her arm and into her heart, April concentrated on the movement of their hands as Ryne ran down the gears preparing to stop the car at the red light ahead. "Shouldn't you be doing that alone?" she asked.

Ryne laughed. When the light turned green, he moved up the gears and gave her finger a gentle squeeze with his thumb before freeing his hand and returning it to the steering wheel. "C'mon, Coach. I'm a team player. There isn't much I like doing alone."

April laughed with him. "You're impossible." She had

another urge to lean closer to him and throw her arm around the back of his seat.

"But likeable, right?"

She looked at him when his gaze left the road again just long enough to lock with hers for a moment. She watched his grin widen and wanted to feel that strong, smiling mouth on hers. A sweet ache centered inside her and, without warning, she realized just how she did feel about Ryne.

"Unfortunately," she admitted.

"Ah, I seem to be making progress. Care to explain?"

April pointed to the brightly illuminated circular driveway ahead on their right. "No time. We're here."

They pulled up to Dr. McKee's sprawling residence at exactly 8 P.M. The single-story home was built entirely of brick with plenty of windows and many well-manicured shrubs surrounding the residence. Pushing on the doorbell, April tried to calm her hammering heart. This was one time when Ryne's presence would help, although she wanted to seal this deal on her own. Guilt gnawed at her because she knew she had invited Ryne for more than just wanting to enjoy an evening out with him. When this evening was over, one way or another, she was going to apologize for using him.

An older man dressed in a starched white jacket and black pants opened the door. April smiled and handed him the invitation.

"Right this way, Ms. Stevens. Sir," he said, nodding at them.

April had been to Aaron McKee's home many times before. The rich interior was distinctly European with rare and expensive rugs covering the highly polished oak floors. She could hear voices and laughter coming from the room to the right and adjusted her smile, hoping to remember the reason she had come despite the warm feeling of Ryne's hand on her back as he escorted her through the doorway.

As soon as April entered, she froze. Coming at her full tilt from three directions were Roger, Jenny and Emily McKee. She fully expected them to run into each other about a foot in front of her and Ryne.

"April dear," Emily said, giving April a quick hug. "Come in. Come in."

April noticed Ryne cover his mouth and cough in an attempt to stifle a grin as Jenny and Roger bumped into each other, stopping just before they would have run over Emily. It was apparently going to be an interesting evening. "Thanks for inviting me, Emily," she said, returning the hug.

Emily straightened. "And this must be Ryne Anderson. Aaron has told me so much about you." She extended her hand. "Welcome to our home."

Ryne took the hand that was offered. He covered it warmly with his. "My pleasure."

"Come and meet our other guests." Emily gestured toward a group of men standing near the fireplace. "A few die-hard Mets fans want to discuss last season with you."

With a quick glance at April, Ryne allowed himself to be led away. Jenny and Roger quickly closed in on April.

"Okay, here's the plan," Jenny said, steering April toward

the bar set in the corner of the room. She plucked two sparkling waters from a tray and handed one to April. "Roger will keep Ryne busy and I'll run interference with you."

"It's okay. I'll be fine," April reassured.

"It's not fine. You. Him. One car. The long ride back to his place after a titillating evening of dining, friends and atmosphere. I can't let that happen. He can find another way home."

"Oops." April grimaced.

"Oops what?" By this time Roger had joined them.

"I let Ryne drive. My car is parked at Roger's."

"No!" Roger set the glass he was holding down. "Now you're at his mercy. No telling where he'll take you later. How did he do it? What did he promise? Diamonds? Gold? The secret to world peace?"

April stifled a grin. "Nothing. It was my idea."

Roger sidled up to her like a undercover agent scooping out a stakeout. "That's how he does it. Makes them think it's their idea and then—wham—they're under his spell." He pulled Jenny by the wrist. "We have to save her."

"What are we to do?" Jenny put the back of her hand to her forehead and feigned helplessness. "I don't know nothin' about savin' anyone," she quipped.

"Okay. I do this all the time. It's been my lot in life to save innocent damsels from Ryne's devastating charm."

Jenny gripped April's shoulders and looked intently at Roger. "You can count on me. Shoot."

Ignoring the questioning stares of some of the guests, Roger pulled the women out into the hall. "They can never be alone during the course of this dinner, and definitely not afterward. You stick to her like glue."

Jenny played along. "Roger, Roger." She shifted her eyes left and right. "And what will you be doing?"

He straightened his tie. "I'll be checking out the food and drink to make sure no one tries to slip her a Mickey."

"And how will we know if someone has tried to do that?"

"Easy. I'll be passed out cold on the floor. If that happens, don't eat or drink what I just did."

As if on cue, Jenny took April's hand and headed in one direction. Roger took off in the other.

From the rear of the room, Ryne had been watching the entire scene. He shook his head and grinned as the trio broke formation. A voice brought him back to the conversation he had been having.

"Do you mean you can't make an 8 A.M. tee-time on Saturday, Ryne?"

Ryne watched Roger come up alongside him. "Yes, of course, Dr. McKee. That'll be fine." He slapped a hand to Roger's shoulder hard enough for the liquid in the glass Roger was holding to splatter onto the rug. "Did I tell you that Roger here has a ten-stroke handicap?" He saw questioning in Roger's eyes and felt suddenly satisfied that he had Roger off-balance for the moment. "He's an ace at chipping out of a sand trap."

"Actually, I'm not that good," Roger protested.

"Nonsense. Don't be so modest," Ryne baited. "You're always in demand for a Pro-Am tournament."

"Is that so?" Dr. McKee turned to Roger. "Perhaps you

can give me some pointers. I seem to always slice that silly ball to the left." He took his stance and swung at an imaginary golf ball at this feet. "Do you think I'm dropping my shoulder?"

As Ryne eased himself away from the group, he saw Roger frantically trying to get away himself. But Dr. McKee's hand firmly on Roger's shoulder held him fast. Ryne lifted his glass in a toast as he caught Roger's eye.

Ryne sipped his drink and laughed. Roger knew nothing about golf. Trying to pretend he did would keep him busy for a while. Turnabout was fair play.

Ryne saw April near the spiral staircase, seemingly involved in conversation with four other women, one of them Jenny. As he approached them, Jenny grabbed April's hand and yanked her toward a larger group of people. He started toward them when Jenny pulled April into the next room.

When he followed, Jenny responded by spiriting April around the corner and out onto the patio. Ryne tried to go after them, but they seemed to disappear into the garden. Flickering torches cast moving shadows on the landscape, making the dimness seem to move and blending the perspective into a dusky setting. It would be impossible to find them without calling attention to himself as he swatted the bushes.

He went back inside. He could wait. Sooner or later they'd get hungry.

Before he could get to April again, the dinner bell rang. Ryne found that he was going to be seated next to Jenny, with Roger next to her and April on Roger's right. With this arrangement, if he were going to talk to her, he'd have to either shout or pass her a note like in high-school study hall. Something was definitely going on. A conspiracy of sorts. He would get to the bottom of it later, but right now he needed a little sleight of hand.

Like a street trickster, he swiped his placard from the plate and switched it with Roger's, firmly planting himself behind the chair, guarding his spot. As the dinner guests found their places, he watched April enter the room. His gaze locked with hers and he felt his smile widen. When she was next to him, he pulled out her chair. With a nod he watched her sit and thought the graceful movement could only be likened to that of a dancer. Dangerous thoughts filled his mind, thoughts of holding her and imagining how they would melt together if they danced.

Through the salad course, he listened to April engage Dr. McKee in general conversation. When the pasta arrived, he noticed her engage some of the guests sitting across from them, and heard her turn the conversation to the Clinic and the advantage of being so close to the New York market.

Despite knowing she disliked this sort of thing, Ryne had to admire her assertiveness and apparent confidence. If she was at all shaky on what she wanted to do, it didn't show. She had smoothly manipulated the conversation to her advantage as though the situation had been scripted.

He was impressed. Very impressed.

They cleared their palates with sherbet and when the main course arrived, the deal seemed to be almost sealed.

He decided to try to make sure of it, not that she appeared to need any help. Maybe he could add something; like an insurance run in a baseball game. Maybe he would even raise his stock a few points in April's eyes.

"I have to agree, Dr. McKee," Ryne said, cutting his filet mignon. "I think the idea of an office in the city is a good one."

McKee's eyebrows rose. "Oh? You were so quiet, I didn't think you were listening." He laughed and a few of the other guests did too.

Ryne grinned. "Don't let the idea of a woman running the thing scare you. April's pretty feisty and goal-oriented. She knows what she wants in life. Don't let that feminine exterior fool you."

April smiled sickly and took a deep breath. She stopped pushing the food around on her plate and narrowed her eyes at Ryne. "Sports rehab is more than just a job to me," she said. "And as long as we're talking about goals," she continued, actually grateful that Ryne had given her the opening she needed, "I really would like to talk to you about the future of Princeton Sports Medicine as I see it. I'd also like to talk to Doctors Quinn and Bledsoe about the concept I would like to put into place over the next few years." She nodded at her dinner partners. "It would be quite an impressive organization."

Dr. Bledsoe's eyebrows rose. "I'm flattered you want my feedback, April."

"I know how important the Clinic is to you, so this must be an important proposal," Aaron McKee noted.

"It is." April glanced at Ryne who nodded slightly as if

in encouragement. "I want you to know that it's more than just an idea. It's more like a mission, one that I would like you to partner with, Aaron."

"I'm intrigued," Aaron said, putting down his fork and resting his wrists on the table, his hands unmoving over his plate. "I know we've talked about this from time to time. Go on."

For the next few minutes April outlined her plan for the satellite office with Aaron McKee spearheading the expansion and having free reign with setting up the New York office. She detailed her contingent plan for instituting a scholarship program for young athletes who could not otherwise afford treatment, taking on at least one case a year and then adding more when viable to do so. When she was through, she held her breath and waited for a reaction after the synopsis.

Dr. Quinn nodded. "I like the idea. But right off the top of my head, I do have a few questions. For one, how long have you been thinking about expanding?"

"For a while now," April replied. She wondered if he suspected that her reasons were as much personal as they were business.

"I think the plan has merit," Roger piped up. "Don't you, Jenny?"

"Yes I do. And I believe April has a blueprint for the proposal back at the office." Jenny turned more fully to April. "Don't you?"

"Well, I'd like to see that. Can you get a copy to me in the morning?" Dr. Bledsoe asked her. "Everyone else interested?"

They all nodded.

"I can have the plans messengered to your offices in the morning. With April's permission, of course," Jenny said.

April felt a little light-headed. The plan was nowhere near polished or ready for serious review. But the ball was rolling and there was no stopping now. "By all means, Jenny."

"I can't promise anything definite right now," McKee cautioned.

"I understand that. And," she said almost breathlessly, knowing the next few minutes might seal the plan, "I'm sure Jenny and I can gather enough data in the next few weeks to see if the idea actually warrants further exploration."

"Not only smart, but reasonable," Ryne added. "A good combination."

April glanced disbelievingly at Ryne before covertly sweeping the napkin from her lap in his direction. As he moved to retrieve it, she dropped her hand and leaned toward the floor. Their hands tussled as they both grabbed the napkin at once. "You can stop it now," she whispered. "I can do this myself."

"I thought I was helping," he replied.

"To a point, but the point is past." She adjusted her position on the chair when they righted themselves. "Thanks," she added, obliging him with a right smile. Power games were something she didn't enjoy.

As the conversation turned to sports in general, her stomach knotted like a huge fist. She prayed the conversation didn't turn to Ryne's progress. More than anything now, she wanted the night to be over.

\* \* \*

With the party winding down, the guests retreated to the study, after-dinner cordials in hand. Jenny positioned herself in front of April. Roger was trying to steer Ryne into another room.

"I'm leaving now, Rog, and I'm taking April with me." Roger began to protest, but Ryne stopped him with a swipe of one hand. "If you try to stop me, I swear I'll tell Aaron McKee that Arnold Palmer is your cousin. How much longer can you bluff about your golf game?"

Trapped, Roger relented. "Okay, but I'm not responsible for anything that happens from this point on."

"I think I can handle it," Ryne replied.

After saying his goodbyes to the hostess, he found April. "How about we get out of here?" he asked.

He was pleased when she nodded her agreement.

April waited until she was in the car until she spoke to him. "What was all that macho stuff in there?"

"What macho stuff?" Ryne asked as he started the car and pulled out of the driveway.

"Oh, don't worry about a woman running the Clinic," April mimicked before punching him on the arm. "Haven't you learned anything? This is a new millennium. That sneaker commercial says it all. This is a woman's world out there. In a lot of cases you guys are just along for the ride."

"Oh really?" Ryne drawled. "You want a ride? You got a ride."

"That's not what I meant and you know it."

He raised his hand as they turned toward the interstate. "Don't try to sweet-talk your way out of this one."

"I have no idea what you're talking about."

"Will wonders never cease. You're almost speechless. Good. Then you won't ask a million questions until we get there."

"What do you have in mind?" April asked.

"Trust me."

"If that's a question, I'm not sure of the answer."

"Good," Ryne replied. He glanced at her and chuckled at the confused look on her face. "Hang on, sweetheart. We're going on a mystery trip."

## Chapter Nine

"What are we doing at the shore?" April asked as they crossed the bridge and headed toward Island Beach.

"Privacy."

Understanding, she settled back into the seat. "I imagine privacy is a precious commodity for you."

"It is. With pre-season about to begin and my rehab not quite finished, the media has been hounding me lately."

"I have been getting some calls," she admitted. "I didn't tell you because I didn't want you to be distracted. I wanted you to concentrate on your therapy."

"I'm not surprised. I figured they'd start coming soon." He flipped on the left signal and turned onto a street that ended at the ocean. "You don't have to tell me what you said, if you're not comfortable."

"No, it's okay. I told them you were progressing through

the regime we set down for you and that you were going to be evaluated shortly."

"Sounds ambiguous."

"It is," she confessed.

"I don't suppose you want to talk about it."

"Actually, no. I'd rather spend the time talking about something safe and neutral."

"And I'd rather not spend the rest of the night with you worrying if I brought you here to debrief you, so let's call it a night on that conversation."

"Sounds like a good idea." April eyed the roadway and noticed that the macadam was about to turn to sand. "We're not taking this thing onto the beach, are we?"

"No," Ryne replied, pointing to his right. "But we can get closer through that street."

He turned onto a partially hidden driveway bordered by sand dunes and winding to the left. It led to an A-frame beach house set back from its nearest neighbor and only a few hundred feet from the water. The garage door opened with a whine as Ryne pushed a button near the car's interior lights. Once inside it slowly closed as automatic lights lit the inside.

"You're full of surprises, aren't you?" She said as he opened the car door and let her out. "Now where?"

"This way." He pulled her to his side, slipping his arm around her and holding it against the small of her back, guiding up three steps and through the unfamiliar house.

The light from the garage sent muted light through the rooms, just enough for her to see her way. She looked at

Ryne as he led her to the living room. She stepped closer to him as she cautiously mirrored his movements and caught the scent of his cologne, a pleasant mixture of herb and lime. She became content to walk with him, enjoying his textures and realizing they drew her far more powerfully than a woman with professional interests in a man ought to admit. She tossed her head to shake her out of her reverie as he stepped away and turned on a light.

The room was spectacular. There were windows on each side of a sliding door facing the ocean, making the whole wall seem to be made of glass. A fireplace faced a large sectional couch that curved gracefully to the right. A center circular staircase broke the room into a living and dining area with the kitchen skillfully hidden behind a partial divider accented with lush plants.

"This is beautiful," she said. She spun in a slow circle, taking in every angle of the large room. "Yours?"

"No. It belongs to The Rockets' owners," Ryne said, circling behind a dark walnut bar. "Sit down. I'll get us something to drink."

"Just some sparkling water," April offered.

"I know I'm only filling in for another man who ran off and left you all alone," Ryne said as ice cubes clinked into glasses he set on the bar top. "But do you think we can pretend this is a real date for a while?"

April shook her head. "I don't think that would be a good idea. And Wil didn't run off. He had a pressing engagement."

Ryne handed her a glass and sat next to her on the sofa. "Your opinion."

"The truth." She whacked her glass down on the coffee table set in front of the sofa. "Let's not talk about Wil, okay?"

"Well, I detect some frost in the air all of a sudden."

"I'd just rather not talk about Wil, if you don't mind."

"I'm sorry. I didn't know you'd be so touchy about that subject."

"I'm not touchy about anything."

"Then why are you pulling your mouth up like a purse string when I mention his name?"

April inhaled and closed her eyes. She forced her facial muscles to relax. Wil's absence did bother her. She knew she had made an impression on Aaron McKee and the other doctors during dinner, but Wil would have been able to get a firm commitment from them all before dessert.

"Truth is, now that the dinner party is over I am a little angry at Wil for not being there."

"You two have a lovers' quarrel about it?"

April snapped her head toward him. "No quarrel and we're not lovers. Let's talk about something else."

"All right, I'm versatile. What do you want to talk about?"

"Something safe," April suggested. "How did you like the dinner?"

"I liked everything except the broccoli."

"I liked everything including the broccoli."

"It figures. Opposites again. So I guess that subject is shot," Ryne said.

"Looks that way."

"This is tough business, this trying to find a common ground," he chided good-naturedly.

April had to smile. "I'll say."

"It's not too bad outside for March. The warm spell is only going to be around for a few more days, so how about we go out onto the deck and enjoy it while we can."

"Only for a minute or two," April agreed. "The breeze blowing off the ocean is sure to be cold and I don't want to get pneumonia."

"That is a little black dress you're wearing. Let me get my jacket." He retrieved his jacket from the stool on which he'd slung it when they first came in and slipped it over her shoulders as they stepped onto the deck.

Outside the moon was at its apex. Silver waves crashed over midnight-colored water onto the shore. The horizon looked endless.

"The view from your deck is much nicer than the one from mine," she said. "Do you come here much to enjoy it?"

"Actually no," Ryne replied, settling his hip onto the rail. "I've only been here a few times over the last few seasons."

Briefly she wondered if he had brought someone with him but resisted the urge to ask. She put her hands on the railing and leaned forward. "I could get lost forever in the way the sky looks as it meets the water. It's beautiful."

Ryne moved closer and curled the fingers of one hand around hers. "I was just thinking the same thing about something else."

His voice was thick and husky. She turned her face to his and saw an emotion that had nothing to do with the scenery flared in his eyes. It was a look she'd seen before. Just as the muscles deep inside her tightened in anticipation, she remembered she shouldn't be alone with him.

"Why are we really here?" she asked.

"I wanted you all to myself for a while."

"But you promised . . . you implied . . . I inferred . . ."
She glared at him. "Never mind."

"The promise I remember making was to myself and it
was that we would have some time together."

"When did you promise that?"

Ryne grinned, remembering the chase at Dr. McKee's
house. "Sometime between the time we got there and the
time Jenny pulled you into the shrubs." He reached across
and ran a finger along the curve of her jaw. "I'm sorry if
I'm giving you the wrong idea, but I'd like to get to know
you better."

"This is really strange, Ryne."

A knowing half-smile played about his lips. "What is?"

"This. You and me actually alone together." Her hand
swept the air. "Looking at this spectacular view from a
beautiful beach house under an exquisite moon. It's turning
into something like a date after all."

"We're not allowed to date," he said firmly, his gaze
roaming over her in obvious appreciation of the way the
moonlight outlined her face in its soft glow. "It's against
the rules."

April was surprised when her heart sank. "Are you
having second thoughts about bringing me here?"

He sighed heavily. "Something like that. Over and over,
the more I see of you, it occurs to me that I want to be
with you as much as possible. It makes me happy to be
with you."

She ignored the tremor that swept though her. "I feel the
same."

"But I also realize that maybe before I do something I regret, I should try some clear-headed thinking."

Suddenly April felt vulnerable and was having some trouble thinking clearly herself. "I don't know what to do, Ryne. Everything gets all confused at times. I want to do what's right for both of us, but sometimes, I just don't know what right is."

Ryne stepped behind her, reached down and put both hands over hers as she gripped the rail. He snuggled his cheek into her hair. "I know. I can't seem to think straight when you're in my arms."

She leaned her head back into his chest. "Neither can I," she admitted quietly. "Maybe it would have been better if we met under different circumstances."

"Maybe."

A silence fell between them and to April it seemed weighed down with regret. It was almost like the last time she'd seen her brother, and she didn't want to face that feeling again.

She laughed to cover her fears. "I bet you can't wait to start hotfooting all over the country to the delight of your adoring fans."

"I don't need the adoration of fans. I need you."

There was no missing the desire behind the words as he spun her in his arms. She swallowed hard and tried to avoid his gaze, but now that she had started the conversation, she knew he'd have no more of her evasive tactics. He held her chin and looked square into her eyes until she could feel the heat from his gaze right down to her toes.

Why did it have to be Ryne who made her feel that way?

"Seems to me that you need someone, too, April."

His low gentle voice brought her senses alive.

"Don't you want someone you can tell whatever is on your mind or whatever is happening to you at the moment without being judged, just being loved?" he continued.

His fingers caressed her cheek and April couldn't look away if she wanted to. Warmth flooded her and she felt right about being with him.

"Ryne, tell me what to do," April said wistfully.

His sudden chuckle cut the tension. "You haven't taken my advice about anything yet. Why would you listen to me now?"

"Because I'm confused. Sometimes, not always mind you," she said, laughing to protect herself from the truth, "I like the way you make me feel and it seems to interfere with my better judgment. A part of me wants more from this relationship, but, and I have to warn you, if the New York branch is a go, I know I'll put all my energies into making it work and I may hurt you."

Ryne stopped touching her and dropped his hand. "You could never hurt me, April."

"I wish I knew that for sure." She raised her hand to touch his cheek this time, but he caught it in midair and stopped her. He gave it a squeeze and let it go.

"It's okay. I can learn to be a patient man while you decide."

"I can't promise you anything. Why would you take the chance of waiting?"

"You're mule-headed, frustrating, occasionally exasperating and sometimes keep me from getting any sleep at all. I find those particularly endearing qualities in a woman."

April stepped back. "Why thank you."

"I'm just trying to focus on your bad points so I won't do something we'll both regret," he said right before he dropped his head and swept her into his arms. "But it's not working."

She could feel his tension. Her head rested against his solid chest, his heart racing in her ear. She tried to tell herself that the overwhelming response she was having inside her heart to being in his arms was only a result of many long months of being without someone in her life.

"This isn't wise," she said.

"People don't always do the wise thing when it comes to feelings."

"You mean people like you and me?"

Ryne nodded. "You give me the self-confidence to admit how I feel."

April smiled. "I never thought of you as lacking confidence of any kind."

"In some areas of my life, it's not a problem. I've always known what I wanted and worked hard to get there. I always felt secure about my personal life, too. That was until I met you. It worries me to think how easily you could slip away from me."

She met his gaze evenly. "I hope not."

"This isn't fair for me to ask you, but I have to know. Do you think this rehab thing could come between us someday?"

April had never been able to avoid honesty, not even when it hurt. "If either of us were forced to make a decision too soon, either personally or professionally, I think it could." His gaze held hers and she saw fear his eyes.

"I pray it never does."

His fingers tangled in her hair and he tilted her face to his. The warmth she felt inside exploded with the emotion she saw in his eyes. Slowly the space between them narrowed until their lips were merely a breath apart and he stopped. He smiled and waited. Her breath caught in her throat and then by her choosing, she began to finish closing the barely visible space between them. Her heartbeat rose in anticipation. That's when she heard the scream.

"Stop before it's too late!"

The urgency in the tone made her snap her eyes open. Her head turned toward the voice just as a bright light was aimed at her eyes. She felt hands tugging at her, ripping her from Ryne's arms.

Shielding her eyes from the shaft of light, she could make out two figures stationing themselves between her and Ryne.

"What are you two doing?" she heard Ryne say. "Turn that thing off."

She heard a metallic click that extinguished the brilliance and momentarily blinded her. It took a few seconds for her eyes to readjust. When they did, she saw Jenny and Roger standing on the deck with her. Now she was really confused.

"Jenny?"

Jenny slapped a hand to her chest. "Thank heavens we got here in time. Who knows what might have happened if we were held up in traffic."

"Nothing," Ryne and April said in unison.

"Yet," Roger chimed in. "But it's pretty obvious to me

that something was starting." He pointed his finger first at Ryne and then at April. "You know that you two have no business being alone together during this sensitive time."

"I told him that," Jenny agreed. "I think we got here just in the nick of time."

"Looks that way," Roger concurred. "You take her, I'll keep him here."

"You are both insane," Ryne insisted. "We're fine."

"When I saw you both leave the dinner party, I thought you might come here," Roger said. "I told Jenny that we had to save April."

"I stand corrected." Ryne squinted at Roger. "Only you are insane. April is perfectly safe here with me."

"Yeah, like all the women in Brooklyn once you turn on the charm."

Ryne swallowed hard, but didn't respond.

"I rest my case," Roger said in triumph, crossing his arms over his chest. "You're speechless." He turned to Jenny. "Let's go with Plan B."

As if caught in a dream, Ryne's disbelieving reaction belied his outward calm. He watched Jenny pull April into the house and toward the garage as Roger put both hands to his chest and held him back.

"Don't take any side trips on the way home," Ryne called out in warning. "I plan on being right behind you. Roger can't keep me here forever."

## Chapter Ten

"Do you know how much it costs for a taxi from Long Beach Island back to here?"

April looked up from the mountain of paperwork she was working on. Roger stood in front of her desk dressed in a jogging suit, arms crossed in front of his chest with a towel draped around his neck.

"Three hundred and forty-six dollars," he said when she lifted her head. "One way."

At first she couldn't imagine what he meant, but he did look serious. She burst out laughing when the situation registered. Ryne must have left him at the beach house.

"Serves you right." She closed the folder she had been reading and straightened in the chair. "What on earth were you two thinking? I thought a bunch of lunatics had broken into the house at first." She pressed her lips together to stifle a grin. "Then there was light in my eyes. Could have

117

been a UFO." She snapped her fingers. "Wait. It *was* a UFO. A couple of them to be exact. Unidentified Flaky Objects."

"Very funny," Roger conceded. He grabbed the ends of the towel with both hands. "Some gratitude. We were saving you, you know."

"A whole lot of people seem to think I need saving." April rolled her eyes. "From what did I need to be rescued this time?"

"Didn't Jenny fill you in on the way back?"

"I wasn't in the mood to talk much." She slid her forearms into the desk and leaned forward. "You broke in at a most inopportune time."

"Exactly. Just in time to save you."

"Save her from what?" Ryne stepped inside the office.

"From you, stud," Roger explained, turning to face him. He turned back to April. "From this poor woman falling prey to some of your masculine wiles."

April felt the heat rise in her cheeks. "You don't have to worry about that, Roger. Ryne must have left his masculine wiles at home. I wasn't falling for any of them."

Ryne angled his watch to Roger's face. "Don't you have a session with Dr. McKee right about now?"

"Yikes. I'm late." Roger dropped into an exaggerated bow. "Be careful, April. He's a charmer."

"Thanks for the advice," April said as Roger disappeared into the hall.

"Thanks for the compliment," Ryne called after him.

"He told me it cost over three hundred dollars to get back from the shore by taxi."

Ryne's eyebrows rose. "Could have hired a limo for that amount and rode in style."

"How could you just leave him there?"

"I really didn't have time to think it through. I grabbed the car keys and left right after Jenny abducted you. I knew he'd find his way home."

"Isn't that a little heartless?"

Ryne shook his head. "His antics at the time seemed a little more so."

"Quite a character," April said, laughing.

"He's harmless."

"I see." April learned long ago that some of the best tactics involved not saying much. She was anxious to get Ryne's take on what had happened the night before.

"Over the past few weeks, you must have come to realize that Roger exaggerates quite a bit."

"Does he now?"

"Masculine wiles? C'mon. Do you really think I have masculine wiles? Whatever they are."

April smiled. "Nice try, but I think we both know what Roger and Jenny were trying to do last night."

"I could use a little help here. I am trying to salvage the moment." He leaned against the doorframe and waited.

April looked at him and decided that Harrison Ford could not have made the innocent gesture look any more masculine. Yes, it appeared that Roger had been right. Ryne did have wiles; very masculine wiles. And she was not immune to the effect they were having on her.

She fumbled with the papers on her desk as he walked over to her. She kept her eyes on his fingers as he took her hands. She laced her fingers with his and allowed herself to be pulled to standing.

It was easy for her to be drawn up into his arms. She inhaled and caught the scent of his aftershave. As her gaze locked with his, her heart mushroomed with such an incredible array of emotions, that all she could do was stare at him for a moment.

"I guess," she said after what she thought was a long period of indecision, "we did have a moment there. Albeit a short-lived one thanks to the interruption."

"Now was that so hard?"

"Not really," April admitted, remembering how she felt right before Jenny and Roger stormed in on them. She didn't want to finish the kiss here in the office, but Ryne made her want to do just that.

Ryne brought her hands to his lips and placed a kiss on each palm. "Do you believe in fate, Ms. Stevens?"

"To a certain extent," April answered. "But I believe more that one can control one's own destiny. Why?" The pounding of her heart lessened as she tried to concentrate on his question.

"Because I do," Ryne replied. "I believe that our lives take off on a certain course and no matter what we try to do to change things, it's beyond our control. I couldn't have stopped myself from hurting my knee if I wanted to. But you see, it had to be so I could come here and meet you."

April peered at him intently. "You could have been less enthusiastic at the celebration in the locker room after winning the World Series. Then you wouldn't have slipped on a wet towel and smashed your knee into a locker."

Ryne took her face between his hands. "It was fate."

She started to say more, then sighed heavily. "So many possibilities," she said with an elusive smile. "For a moment there I almost forgot I was the owner and you were the client." She was torn. A few minutes more and she might have confided her feelings to him. She sensed his need to talk, but she knew she would regret it later. She slipped her fingers beneath his hands and removed them from her cheeks. "I think we could have been good together if we had the chance."

"We still can be." A hopeful smile played around his lips.

"I have a meeting," April said, swallowing the lump that was forming in her throat. She squeezed his hand. "I shouldn't be late."

"No. I suppose you shouldn't." His tone was skeptical. He winked and vanished into the hallway.

It was only after April let out the breath she was holding that she realized the thought of meeting with Dr. McKee was suddenly making her very nauseous.

"I'm afraid," Aaron McKee said to the people surrounding the oval table with noticeable regret tinting his voice, "that Ryne Anderson isn't coming along as fast as I had hoped that he would."

Tommy Williams, who had been leaning back in one of the leather chairs, snapped upright, his jaw hanging. "I was afraid you were going to say something like that."

McKee directed his attention to Coach Williams. "The knee's getting stronger, but very slowly."

April moved uncomfortably in her chair. A few hours earlier she had peeked at Ryne's chart. She hadn't liked the notes Aaron made in the margins on some of the papers. She flinched inwardly, knowing that he would be a bear if she questioned him too much.

Aaron McKee was the best in the field. If anyone could get Ryne back on the baseball diamond, McKee was the man. He was also the man she wanted for the New York office and he hadn't given her a definite answer to the proposal. She was walking a fine line and she knew it.

Ryne was healing, but healing slowly. From what she deduced from the test results and Aaron's notes, Ryne wouldn't be ready to join his team by opening day. She ardently avoided talking to him about his progress and he carefully avoided bringing up the subject when they talked.

But she knew that wouldn't be the case much longer. Especially after this meeting.

"But," Williams sputtered, after a moment of silence. "Pre-season starts in two weeks. Anderson *has* to be there."

Fingers tightening around the pencil in her right hand, April intervened. "Aaron, can you elaborate? I've read the charts, but I'd like to hear it from you." She tensed further, watching Aaron's set features.

"I'm not going to mince words," McKee said. "We all knew this was a very serious injury. Originally the MRI showed a tear to the medial meniscus just between the anterior curciate ligament and the medial collateral ligament that sits behind the kneecap."

Williams raised both hands in a defensive pose. "Whoa. I knew he banged up his knee and I knew that it would be a long road back, but I'm no med student here. In English, please."

McKee edged his chair closer to the coach's and pulled a pen from his coat pocket. He sketched a quick diagram loosely resembling a human leg. "Sudden twisting such as what happened when Anderson fell and hooked his leg on the bench in the locker room often pinches the meniscus, the joint cushion between the femur and the tibia."

Williams nodded and stared at the drawing, studying it with interest.

"When that happens, the cartilage splits and rips open. In his case, it was complicated further by an old tear becoming re-injured. We had to clean out a lot more than we originally anticipated. Now I've noticed an increase in scar tissue when I read the last MRI a few days ago. It means he could have slightly re-injured the area by pushing too hard."

Williams' mouth grew tight as he remembered talking to the owner about the time Ryne was on the disabled list for a month when he played triple-A ball. It happened right before the team called him up to the majors. Ryne had tried to catch a pop fly in foul territory and ran right into the visiting dugout, slamming his knee on the bench. He fought his way back from that injury, but that was a long time ago and this one seemed a whole lot more serious.

A muscle clenched along his jaw line and he searched the emotionless face of the doctor for even the slightest ray of hope. "Then what you're saying is that Anderson is through with baseball."

"That's not what I'm saying. Exactly. Still, I'm also not promising that it isn't going to happen, either."

"Can't you just do some more laser surgery and clean it up?"

"It's not quite that simple. Laser surgery would be a quick fix, but it could have additional complications down the line. If we remove all or part of the damaged meniscus and the forming scar tissue, even more might form to help pad the joint. The scar tissue doesn't cradle the bones as well as a healthy meniscus and 'wear and tear' arthritis may develop. At best Anderson might need additional surgery at the end of the season. At worst, he could be facing post-traumatic arthritis or osteoarthritis."

"I see."

"That's why we tried to avoid doing more than necessary and went with some additional rest and natural healing right after the surgery. I didn't want to rush into physical therapy. Some team owners and coaches wouldn't have agreed, but I felt this was the way to go."

Slipping both hands behind his head and moving his eyes to look up at the ceiling, Williams leaned back in his chair and let out a long sigh before speaking. "C'mon, Doc. Bottom line. Can Anderson play ball or not?"

Dr. McKee paged through his notes and mulled over the tough question. Thirty-one is about middle age for a ball player and it had been widely publicized that Ryne, in the last year of his contract with the New York Rockets, was looking for a new multi-year deal complete with a hefty raise in salary or he'd walk.

It was also common knowledge that a few hotshot rookies in the Rockets' minor league system were waiting for Ryne to lose his edge so they could get their shot at filling his position on the baseball diamond. It all boiled down to a whole lot of pressure when it came time for Ryne to make the decision to either prove himself after such a severe injury or pack it in and let his career turn to diamond dust if he failed.

On the plus side, Ryne was in excellent physical condition except for the knee injury. And he did love baseball. Sometimes determination was ninety percent of an athlete's recovery process.

"Truthfully, whether he plays again or not is going to take some more time for me to evaluate properly," Dr. McKee finally said.

April took a breath and held it, watching the coach. The urge to jump in and tell McKee he was wrong was very real. But she saw the test results and she knew better.

Slowly she released her breath. This showdown had been coming for a long time. She had tried every conceivable way she knew to make the results come out different, but no matter how she tried to interpret them, the conclusion was the same.

"Can we give him another week to ten days and then re-evaluate before sending in a final report?" she asked hopefully.

McKee shook his head. "I don't think that a week will change anything. Anderson needs about another six weeks in rehabilitation and another round of testing before I can re-evaluate and even think about releasing him."

"Geez, then there's another six weeks or so for him in the minors to see if the knee holds up," Williams said, raking his hand through his salt-and-pepper hair. "The press is going to have a field day with this one. Not to mention that my butt is on the line with the owner. I swore that Anderson would be back on the first day of practice."

"I'm sorry that it turned out this way. People heal differently. The textbooks give us an approximate, but you just don't know until you start the rehab." McKee looked almost apologetic.

April closed her eyes. She knew he was right. "Let's take this one step at a time. We know Ryne's healing. Just not as fast as we or the team would like him to."

"That's about it," McKee agreed.

April turned to Williams. "And the team can start preseason without him, can't they?"

"We'd rather not."

"And we'd rather not release a patient until he or she was totally ready." April was suddenly aware of nothing but the widening pain in her heart over the realization that she was going to have to tell Ryne that his career was on hold for a while.

"What do I tell the owner? Erhart is going to go ballistic when he hears this."

"Would you like me to tell him?" April offered. "I have some experience dealing with people who are not quite ready to hear the reality of a situation."

For a brief moment a fist closed around her heart and squeezed with her words. Her thoughts shifted from Ryne to her brother. She hadn't done such a good job then. She swore this time it would be different.

Williams waved his hands in the air. "No. I'll do it. It's

part of my job. But let me talk to Erhart first, before you say anything to Anderson. I'd like to get some options before I lay this one over the plate for Anderson to swing at. Maybe I can soften the blow a little."

"Fair enough," April said. "Then we can meet and talk with Ryne."

Williams began to stand and then dropped back into the chair. He slapped a hand to his forehead and let out a long breath of air. "Geez, I almost forgot. What about the press? A few sportswriters would love to get their hands on a story like this."

April thought for a moment. "If someone leaks the story, I'll handle the press. By then I hope Ryne will have agreed to a course of action. We'll tell everyone he's coming along and leave it at that."

"What about the follow-up questions?" Williams protested. "If we don't give out some solid facts, the media will most likely speculate about what's happening to a poster-boy star like Anderson and what the team is going to do about it."

"You'll have to handle the baseball side. This clinic can only advise you when Ryne will be ready. How the Rockets management reacts to the time frame is not for me to say."

"And who'll explain the reason for the delayed decision? The media is smart enough to figure out that someone should have known something a whole lot earlier than this."

Clearing her throat April gave a jerky nod. "Don't worry. I'll protect the confidentiality we agreed upon."

"What about when some hotshot reporter pushes you for

a final decision?" Williams pressed. "Who do you protect then?"

"In that case," April said, rising and placing both hands on the table for emphasis, "I will be there to protect both the New York Rockets and Ryne Anderson."

## Chapter Eleven

During the following few hours April learned things about stressing that she'd never known before. Worrying about Ryne, the Clinic, and her future was pulling her in all directions at once.

At one point, she actually thought it might be possible to cry herself to death because of the frustration she was feeling. She spent the good part of the afternoon alternately teary-eyed, running for the tissue box, but then chiding herself for acting so unprofessionally.

To make matters worse, Ryne called asking if he could see her later, forcing her to lie about being tied up for the rest of the day.

And then Wil called, saying he was back from Europe and taking a private jet from Newark International to Princeton. He wanted April to pick him up at the local airport. He said he had something important for her and it couldn't wait. She closed her eyes and sighed.

"Why can't he take a limo?" she said aloud.

"Why can't who take a limo?"

April looked up to see Jenny standing in the doorway.

"Sorry, I didn't realize I said that out loud. It's Wil. He wants me to pick him up at Princeton Airport."

"I agree then. Let him take a limo."

"I've already committed. We're going to an early dinner at The Manor. He said he had something important to ask me."

"Oooh, if I didn't know better, I'd say he was getting serious."

"That's all I need right now."

Jenny walked to an empty chair and dropped herself into it. "So I guess then you've told Ryne about the setback. How'd he take it?"

April's eyes widened. "No, I didn't. Not yet. How do you know about it anyway?"

"Dr. McKee's assistant is out today. He asked me if I could help out and type up a few notes he needed. I read as I type, you know. April, what are you going to do?"

"I don't know."

"You have to tell him."

She closed her eyes. A terrible pain shot across her heart. "The Rockets coach, Tommy Williams, is discussing Ryne's situation with the team owner tonight in New York. He's planning on filling Erhart in on Ryne's progress and Dr. McKee's conclusions. First thing in the morning, we're all meeting to tell Ryne the news and discuss the remainder of his rehabilitation. Then, I suspect, Ryne will meet privately with Williams and Erhart to discuss his future with the team." She opened her eyes. "It's not good, Jenny. He may not play again."

"You know, it's going to look like you've sided with the team. Are you sure that's how you want it to be?"

"What choice do I have?"

"You can tell him first, this afternoon, before it seems like everyone is ganging up on him."

"That's not a very professional thing for me to do. It could cost me everything I've worked for so far."

"Not if you stay focused on what's right for his health and help him get through it. We both know there's something special going on there between you two. He's going to need you."

April leaned back in her chair. She put her hands on her forehead, trying to stop the pain that was building. "I want to tell him that it's not the end of the world, that it's just going to take a little more time than we thought it would. I should assure him that he can do this, that we will do it together."

"So what's the problem then?"

"It's happened awfully fast; these feelings I have. I need some time to make sure what I feel is not connected to my desire to make this clinic work. I've waited a long time to find the right man. I don't intend to make a temporary commitment if I finally do make one."

"I know that," Jenny said.

"And what about Ryne? His career is everything to him. Maybe he will hate me for having to bring it to a possible early end."

"He won't hate you, April."

April shifted her gaze to the ceiling before shoving her chair away from her desk and stood. She walked over to the window and stared out. "I want to do the right thing. There are so many people depending on this decision."

Jenny joined her at the window. She arched an arm around April's shoulders.

"What about you, April? Who do you depend on?" She turned April around and looked straight into her eyes. "You won't let anyone down if you do the right thing for Ryne *and* follow your heart for yourself."

April sighed and then laughed. "Heaven help me, I love him." It was such a relief to say it aloud at last. "Does everyone go through such agony when they finally admit they've met 'the one?'"

"Only those who try to deny the truth."

"I always thought that when I found the guy that was right for me, bells and whistles would go off, and it would be so perfect. There'd be no problems, no complications, we'd simply ride off into the sunset on his white horse to our castle and live happily ever after."

"Well," Jenny said, putting her arm back around April's shoulders. "The white horse is really a silver Audi, the castle is an apartment in Manhattan, and the complication for you is the New England Blue-Blood who is expecting a ride from the airport and has the hots for you."

"The real problem is telling Ryne he can't play ball for another few weeks, maybe months." She began to walk to the door. "I should be the one to tell him, even if it means a lecture on accountability from Dr. McKee in the morning."

"Wait," Jenny called out, pointing to the parking lot outside the window. "You've missed your chance. He's leaving. Best thing you can do now, if you're sure you want to do this, is call him on his cell phone and ask him to meet you back here."

April dropped her shoulders. "Do you think he suspects anything?"

"Honestly, no."

"How can you tell?"

Jenny pointed to Ryne's car. "He's doing the speed limit. I would suspect that if a man like him had just found out that his career was in jeopardy, all you'd see is a cloud of smoke and a silver streak."

As April waited for Wil's plane to land, she tried Ryne's cell number again. After five rings, his voice said, "You know what to do," followed by a beep.

If that were only true, April thought as she left him yet another message to call her.

She couldn't reach Aaron McKee either. She wanted to tell him of her decision to talk to Ryne. She could leave him a message, but felt it was important to talk to him directly and not take the coward's way out.

Just as she began to dial Ryne's number again, Wil came up on her left.

"I'm back," he announced.

"How was your flight?" April flipped her cell phone closed tucking it into the tray on the center console.

"First-class is always wonderful. Getting through customs takes longer with all the extra security. But I don't mind if it makes the skies safer." He put down his carry-on and touched her arm through the open car window. "I do have some wonderful news to tell you."

She pointed to the passenger seat. "Get in." She waited until he was seated. "Tell me the news and it better be good. I could use something other than gloom and doom right now."

"Where's April?"

Jenny looked up from the information she was reading on the new aerobic dance program she was thinking of fitting into the schedule.

"Hey, Ryne," she said, greeting him with her brightest smile. "She went to pick up Wil at the airport."

Ryne dropped into the chair opposite the desk. "The rich guy couldn't take a cab?"

"That's exactly what I thought."

"When's she coming back?"

"Didn't she call you?"

"I forgot to replace the battery on my cell phone."

"She's not coming back here. They're having dinner."

"Oh?"

"Wil said he had something important to ask April."

Ryne leaned back in the chair and crossed his legs, right ankle on left knee.

"Careful," Jenny warned.

"Right knee's the bad one." He entwined his fingers over his midsection. "Something important, huh? Any ideas?"

Jenny shook her head. "Never can tell with Wil. Could be business, could be personal. He's been in love with her for years, you know."

A warning light went off in Ryne's head. He uncrossed his legs and leaned forward, interested.

"No, I didn't know, although I suspected something like that. Should I be worried about anything?"

"Possibly," Jenny blurted out, forgetting for a moment that Ryne was talking about Wil. She was thinking more about what Ryne faced in the morning.

The look on Ryne's face changed to one of concern. She struggled with the way she could answer his question yet not tell him what she knew. She felt awful about having to technically deceive him, but knew she had no choice. It wasn't her call. It was April's.

"I don't know for sure that something's going to happen. Wil's normally not one to do anything drastic." She tried hard to sound calm, but felt that warm rush people get when they lie. "But nothing about this situation has been normal from the beginning."

"Jenny, you worry me sometimes."

"Funny, I worry me all the time."

Ryne stood and started for the door. "So where did you say they were going for dinner."

"I didn't."

"But you will."

Jenny thought for a moment before deciding it wouldn't do any harm to tell him. April did want to see Ryne. Maybe not with Wil around, but she had to see him soon.

"The Manor," Jenny volunteered. "It's out by the college."

"I'll find it," Ryne said. "I have this sudden craving for take-out."

\*   \*   \*

Wil signaled for the waiter to bring him another wine. "April, you haven't heard one thing I've said since I got in the car."

"I have a lot on my mind."

"We should order soon," Wil said nodding to the waiter. He deftly turned the wine bottle so it wouldn't spill onto the white damask tablecloth. "Or else I may have too much wine and let someone take advantage of me later."

"No one ever takes advantage of you, Wil. You're much too shrewd a businessman to let something like that happen."

He reached over and patted April's hand. "I've been thinking a lot about the future."

"You have?"

Wil nodded. "I met many seasoned European men on my trip. They told me the best way to handle a woman, was to simply love her and accept her as she is."

First Ryne, now Wil. What was it about men that made them think dinner and romantic suspense was what a woman wanted? She was beyond falling into some sort of macho male trap.

"And how am I?" April turned the page on the menu, forcing Wil to move his hand. She looked at the page, but the selections blurred, as the ache in her head grew stronger. She needed Wil to get to the point and not try to do a scene from Camelot.

"How's the salmon here?" She squirmed in the seat hoping Wil would let his comment drop.

"You're changing the subject, aren't you?"

"I suppose I am," April affirmed, snapping the menu shut with both hands. "Why don't you just tell me what this is all about."

"Let's order first. I'm famished."

"Didn't you eat on the plane?"

"Airplane kitchens are not five-star restaurants, darling. I never eat airline food. I'd rather starve."

The waiter returned and April re-opened the menu, making a quick uninvolved selection. She waited until Wil ordered before continuing.

"Are you sure the chef here doesn't work for an airline on the side?" She asked.

Wil gave her an apathetic nod. "Yes. This place was profiled in *New Jersey Magazine* as one of the ten best restaurants in the state, otherwise what would be the point of coming here at all?"

"Wil Tyler, you are such a snob."

"No, I'm not," he protested.

"Be careful," April said, laughing. "Or the silver spoon you have in your mouth will fall out and you'll lose it under the table."

## Chapter Twelve

Ryne pulled up to the front door of The Manor, got out of the car and tossed the keys to the valet. "Keep it close, I'll be right out."

He'd never been to this particular restaurant before and had a hard time finding it. On a side street with access through a winding driveway, The Manor was a converted mansion boasting elegant dining and old-world ambience, making it a perfect gathering place for the society of Princeton.

As Ryne approached the beveled lead glass front door, it swept open. A white-gloved member of the staff greeted him warmly. "Good evening, sir. Are you joining a party for dinner?"

"Yes," Ryne replied, feeling like an intruder. "Some friends of mine are already here."

"Please see the host to your right." The attendant swept

his hand toward the rear of the entrance hallway. "Robert will have someone escort you to the table."

As he walked to the rear of the richly carpeted entrance hall, Ryne felt uncharacteristically out of place. An ornate fireplace with a marble mantel took up most of the left wall. Deep brown leather chairs and tables with matching marble tops dotted the room. A crystal chandelier reflected light in a hundred directions and the sound of a concerto quietly filled the air as a virtuoso shared his talent with patrons in an adjoining banquet room. A few diners, women in gowns and men in tuxedos, passed him, nodding mechanically as they entered the banquet area. This was definitely Wil Tyler territory.

He could picture April being equally as comfortable rubbing elbows with society. If he closed his eyes, he could see her dressed in silk, poised on the arm of a tuxedo-clad diplomat waiting for the curtain to rise at Lincoln Center.

Ryne looked down at his navy sports jacket. Although black-tie events were not foreign to him, and many sought him out for friendship or endorsement, it wasn't his lineage or distinction that drew the attention. It was his status as a star baseball player that opened doors for him. At this moment, the door he'd rather have opened was one to a sports bar.

He blew out a long breath. Maybe he should have gone to college instead of the minors.

A well-dressed couple emerged from one of the elegant dining rooms on other side of the hall.

"Ryne Anderson, isn't it?" The man said, extending his hand.

Ryne grasped it firmly. "Yes." He smiled an acknow-
ledgment. "Nice you meet you."

"My grandson has posters of you all over his room," the
man continued.

"I'm surprised," Ryne replied. "I thought this was Phil-
lies country."

"Not for him. The boy's a real Rockets fan. He's been
following your career for a while now. He'll be disappointed that he wasn't here to meet you. He's been following your progress in the papers. He's recovering from a
sports injury now too. I think he relates to you that way."

"I hope it wasn't too serious."

"No. Skiing accident. But kids are resilient. He's going
to be fine. He just got the cast off his leg and was pro-
nounced physically able to play by the orthopedist. You
know how quickly kids can shake off that sort of thing.
My grandson is really looking forward to little league in
the summer."

"Glad to hear it," Ryne said, feeling a twinge of envy.
Kids were so resilient. He wished his thirty-one-year-old
bones and muscles would recover as quickly.

"Yes, he's going to be mighty upset that I met you and
he didn't. I take him to as many games as I can in New
York. He skis because he can't play ball in the snow. Tried
like heck for months to talk his grandmother and me into
buying a house in Florida so he could play ball all year
long. That's how much he loves baseball."

Ryne grinned. He could relate to that feeling. "I may
have a promo picture in the trunk of my car. Do you think
he'd like it?"

"I don't want to hold you up. I'm sure you're a very busy man."

"When I was your grandson's age, I felt that same way about baseball as he does," Ryne said. "I would have been thrilled if my grandfather brought me home a signed picture of a professional baseball player as a surprise one day. But we lived on a farm in the middle of nowhere, so the best he could do was bring me pictures of the John Deere salesmen."

"You're going to make me a real hero with my grandson."

"I'll bet you're already his hero," Ryne said, walking with the couple to the door. "My car's right outside. Let's get that picture for him."

"That photo will definitely ensure me the title," the man said, smiling broadly.

Even as a strange feeling of angst crept over him, Ryne knew he was doing the right thing. He made it a point never to turn down an opportunity to do something for the fans, especially kids. He didn't think much of sports stars who got caught up in the fortune and glory and lost track of what was really important.

His quest to find April would have to wait a little while longer.


"So that's why I'm moving to Austria for the next year."

April stopped cutting her filet mignon and slowly raised her gaze to meet Wil's. "What did you say?"

"I'm moving to Europe for a while."

The sterling silver fork dropped from April's hand. She

caught it as it grazed the edge of the fine china plate with a melodic tinkle. Carefully she set it aside.

"But the Clinic is at a critical stage. You can't leave. I need you to help me sew up the deal with the New York office and Aaron McKee."

Wil brushed her plea away with a slight swipe of his hand. "Nonsense. You don't need help from anyone to finish the deal." Wil waited until the white-jacketed wine waiter refilled the crystal goblet to the perfect level and set the bottle back into the silver ice bucket on the stand next to the table. "What I have always admired about you the most, April, has been your fire and determination. But those qualities are also the things that have kept you from needing me as much as I would have liked you to."

April looked down at the maroon linen napkin on her lap and felt a strange feeling fill her. Wil finally admitted they were only ever going to be friends. She almost felt as though she had let him down.

"Wil," she said, lifting her chin to meet his gaze. "Your move to Europe, it isn't because we never will be—"

"Don't even say it." He reached over and pressed his forefinger to her lips. "I must admit, I was tempted to try to blackmail you into a relationship but I knew it wouldn't work." He sat back and smiled. "You tried to tell me for years that nothing could happen between us. I refused to listen."

April caught Wil's gaze. She visibly relaxed when she saw nothing more than sincere friendship in his eyes. She turned on her smile. Wil's own smile returned.

"I feel like I'm losing my best friend," she said.

"That will never happen. We'll always be close."

"I'll worry about you over there. It's a really unpredictable time."

"You don't have to worry about me. I pretty much know my way around Vienna and I have met someone interesting."

April felt her eyes widen. "Really?"

"A Countess actually."

"Royalty." She put her elbow on the maroon tablecloth and set her chin in her palm. "I am intrigued. Tell me everything."


Ryne said his good-byes and returned to the restaurant. Choosing not to enlist the help of the maître d', he began to weave his way through the smaller dining rooms each holding just four or five tables.

Trying to be as inconspicuous as possible, he kept to the edges, ducking behind large plants strategically placed to either add to the character or hide an awkward corner when necessary. Convinced that the time he spent outside caused him to miss her, Ryne prepared to give up the search when he saw April.

She and Wil were sitting at a table in the last dining room near a large window overlooking the rear gardens. She was leaning forward, her chin resting on her entwined fingers, apparently totally captivated with whatever Will was saying. The crystal accents on the table seemed to capture light from the flickering candles and release it into her eyes, making them sparkle even from a distance.

As Wil continued to speak, April's smile grew wider and

she became more animated. Even from a distance Ryne could see Wil's face reflecting satisfaction and exhilaration.

That was not good, Ryne decided. His first thought was to rush in and break up whatever was going on. His second was being thrown out of an elite restaurant for causing a scene in front of the woman he was trying to win over. Instead, he slipped behind a potted palm and spread the fronds. He'd wait and try to find out exactly what was going on before he made his move.

"And that's how I met her," Wil said. "We spent most of the past week together. She's quite delightful. Not as much fun as you, but charming nonetheless."

"If you marry her will you be a Count then?" April asked, a teasing tone shading her voice. "Count Wilton Tyler III. I suspect I'd have to throw myself at your feet and lower my eyes when we met. Or would a curtsy do? And do you think she would want a large diamond if you two got serious? There is a five-caret Champagne Tyler Diamond I've heard so much about. Of course I've never actually seen it, but it is legendary. Family heirloom, I believe. In a safe in Switzerland, right? So you could just jump in a Benz you'd buy there and drive across Europe to get it."

Wil leaned forward in the chair. "Are you trying to get rid of me by marrying me off to a woman I just met so you can run the bases with your baseball hero?"

Wil looked wounded. She reached out and touched his hand. "I'm not running the bases with anyone, especially not Ryne. I'm not sure how I feel about him." She was lying and she knew it, but now was not the time to talk about another man and the confused jumble of feelings he evoked whenever she was with him. "But I know how I feel about you. You're very special to me. You always will be." She squeezed his hand fondly before sitting back in her chair.

"I feel the same way." He dabbed at the corners of his mouth with the napkin and sat back in the chair. "You know I asked you here for a reason."

His tone was suddenly more serious than April would have liked it to be. She felt suddenly uneasy. "What are you going to do, Wil?"

"Although I am planning on getting to know the Countess better," Wil replied, standing, "there is one thing I need to do first. Just to be sure." He reached to his inside jacket pocket and produced a black velvet box.

April felt all the color drain from her face and a wave of nausea gripped her. "Wil, stop. Don't say another word."

He dropped to one knee. "April, if you will accept this, you'd make me the happiest man on the face of the earth." He angled the box toward her and slowly opened the lid.

April's eyes widened and for a moment she felt light-headed enough to faint. She looked from the box to Wil and saw the expression on his face change. Leaping from her chair, she pulled him to standing and threw her arms around his neck as the onlookers burst into applause.

"Can I help you sir?"

For a moment Ryne didn't react to the words or to the confused waiter who peered at him through the fern fronds.

His ears thundered with the sound of the diners clapping. His gaze was focused on the velvet box in Wil's hand, the contents catching the light and sparkling like a brilliant star.

Or a perfect diamond.

"Sir, are you all right?" The waiter's voice rose, attracting the attention of a few guests at nearby tables. He stood in the archway leading to the room in which Wil and April were dining and, for all intents and purposes, probably looked like he was talking to a plant.

Ryne reached around the fern and pulled the waiter out of April's sight line. "No. Yes. No." He gave his head a quick shake to clear the fog that formed inside. "Honestly, I'm not sure."

"Is something wrong?"

Ryne looked past him into the dining room. Wil and April had sat back down and were now looking toward the doorway. Grabbing him by the shoulders, Ryne pulled the waiter behind the plant. The young man did a quick juggling act to keep a pitcher of mineral water and some glasses from tumbling to the floor. A few people nearby frowned in disapproval. One motioned to a passing busboy.

"I just need to stay here for a few more minutes," Ryne explained, steadying the crystal pitcher as it wobbled on the serving tray.

"I don't think you can," the young man replied.

"Randolph, is there a problem?" another voice inquired.

Ryne turned his head to the right in time to see the headwaiter fast approaching. He turned back and checked the far dining room through the fern blades. Wil had apparently decided to check on the disturbance and was coming at him from the left.

If Ryne didn't do something fast, he'd be trapped between the wall and the potted palm. He started to move past the astonished waiter and it became a dance. The waiter tried to balance the tray as Ryne tried to get out of the corner. They spun in a few circles before gravity and momentum won and the contents of the tray crashed onto the floor. All heads turned toward the sound.

Grabbing the tray from the bewildered waiter, Ryne flipped it on end and held it in front of his face. As he made a mad dash for the exit, he ran squarely into the headwaiter, the force spinning the man around and depositing him into the lap of an older woman dining with four friends. A few patrons stood in response to her shriek.

Ryne never looked back. He tossed the tray Frisbee style to the maître d', hit the door running and burst through. He saw his car parked near the fountain in the front of the restaurant and signaled the valet for his keys.

Never breaking stride, he caught them with one hand and was in the car and gone before the headwaiter made it out to the parking lot.

"Wasn't that Ryne Anderson?" the man asked, as he watched the silver car race down the driveway with a squeal of its tires.

"Yes," the parking attendant replied. "And he didn't even tip me."

As the commotion died down, Wil returned to the table. He slipped the linen napkin back onto his lap and took a small sip of wine.

"What was that all about?" April asked, as the excitement died down and the busboy cleared the floor.

"A stalker, I think."

"You're kidding. In here?"

"Apparently one of the waiters caught a man hiding in the plants watching someone in this room."

April glanced at the other diners. "Wonder who?" Her gaze settled on a model-perfect blond at a corner table. "I bet it was her. I see that she's here with an older man. Bet she dumped her college sweetheart for him, and the spurned lover came here to get her back."

Wil dismissed the premise with a wave of his hand. "Very B-movie, but that's Samantha Edgar and she's here with her father. Sam's husband is in Japan cementing a big electronics deal. Everyone knows they're very happy."

"Won't you miss all this society gossip when you move to Europe?" April asked, smiling.

Wil's face became serious. "No, I'll miss you."

Her smile softened. "And I'll miss you." She looked at his sad smile. "Wil, I do love you, but as a friend. Nothing will ever change that. I'll always be there for you, and I know that I'll be able to always count on you. Sometimes that's the best kind of love."

"Friends." Wil's voice seemed almost melancholy as he turned the velvet box around and around in his hand. "I suppose you're right." He face brightened. "But admit it, I had you there for a few minutes, didn't I?"

April picked up the velvet box. "You *scared* me there for a few minutes."

"You looked positively awful."

"Bad clams."

"I don't think so." Wil pumped his hand in triumph. "I got you. After all these years, I finally got you."

As April opened the box, light again caught the facets of the contents, reflecting tiny shafts of perfect sparkle. She heard Wil smother a laugh. "If I ever get lonely or sentimental while you're jet-setting around Europe and rubbing elbows with royalty, I'll just put on these earrings and think of you."

"Finest Austrian crystal," Wil said in a satisfied tone. "Worth every cent I paid to see the look of sheer panic on your face." His grin grew wider. "And that's what I'll remember from now on every time I think of you."

## Chapter Thirteen

The front door crashed open so hard that the pictures on the office wall rattled and nearly fell to the floor. Roger jumped up from the computer and closed the distance to the living room in just a few strides. There he saw Ryne peel off his sports coat and throw it onto the sofa as though he was trying to make a play at first base.

"Geez, Anderson, did you leave the hinges on the door?"

Ryne gave him a critical look and continued to struggle with his tie. "Don't let me interrupt whatever you were doing."

"Interrupt? You crashed through the front door so hard that I couldn't hear myself E-mail in the office."

"Roger, I have more important things to do right now than worry about your chat-room adventures."

Roger walked over to the front door and pulled it away

150

from the wall. The doorknob had put a hole right through the sheetrock. "Like redecorate?"

Ryne reached over to the bookcase, grabbed a baseball from the top shelf and shoved it into the hole. "There. Now we have a doorstop."

"What gotten into you?"

"Nothing." Ryne stormed into the kitchen. He opened the kitchen faucet wide open. Putting his hands on the sink, he leaned forward and just watched the water run. "Listen, I'm just having a bad day."

"Have you done something I should know about? The knee okay?" Roger asked, walking to Ryne and putting a hand on his shoulder.

"It's fine." Ryne let the water fill his cupped hands. He splashed his face in a sobering attempt to clear his head.

Roger reached around him and turned off the water. "You're sure acting as though someone signed your execution papers. Something up with the knee?"

Ryne dropped his head and turned. Water droplets glistened on his skin. "Listen, the knee is the least of my worries right now."

"Talk to me, man."

He glanced up at Roger through narrowed eyes. "I think April just got engaged to the computer nerd."

Roger's mouth fell open. They stared at each other for a while. "You think she did or you know she did?"

Shaking his head in exasperation, Ryne walked away and began to pace. "Saw the guy on his knee with a little box in his hand. Then April threw her arms around his neck and the people in the restaurant started clapping. What more do I need? An invitation to the wedding?"

Roger let out a low whistle. "Great." He looked at Ryne. "I guess you hadn't gotten around to telling her how you feel about her."

He stopped dead in his tracks. "No, and I don't think it will make any difference now."

Ryne sat in the dark in the living room replaying the evening in his mind. If he hadn't taken the time to sign autographs, maybe he could have stopped it.

He closed his eyes and shook his head. No, he couldn't disappoint the gentleman's grandson. Ryne wasn't made that way.

Seize the moment, his mother always told him. Don't waste an opportunity or someone else would take it from you. That's how he got as far as he had in baseball. Stepping up when the team needed a big hit. Grabbing that screaming line drive when the team needed the final out.

He still had a chance to tell April how he felt about her when he first saw her and Wil at the table. He should have walked right in and said something before Wil had time to whip out that little velvet box.

But he'd hesitated. For the first time in his life he didn't follow his gut feeling and it cost him.

He sighed heavily and leaned forward. Resting his forearms on his thighs, he let his head drop. He and April just weren't meant to be, he guessed. Maybe he could still do something or say something to change things. Maybe there was still time.

He started to rise, but sat back down heavily. April was engaged now. How could he ask her to give the ring back to Wil just because he wanted her? How could he put her in that position? He couldn't do that to her. It wouldn't be right. If April were going to change her mind about marrying Wil, it would take a miracle at this point.

But he couldn't afford to believe in miracles anymore. He had to concentrate on having a good year with the Rockets. No, he'd have his *best* year ever with the Rockets. Winning another world championship at the end of the season would help him forget what he lost before the season ever began.

This was not the time in his career to start trusting in miracles. Baseball was the only thing he could hold onto now.

"So that's it? It's that cut and dry?" Tommy Williams bolted to standing and strode away from Dick Erhart.

"Anderson is in his option year. We'll buy out the rest of his contract. He'll be fine."

"No he won't. He's not playing just for the money. He's one of the few guys left who still loves the game."

Erhart put his drink down on the cherry wood coffee table and got up. He put his hands up in supplication. "Tommy, what can I do? I have a championship to defend."

Tommy strode back to the Rockets' owner and glared at him. Nose to nose, he waited until Erhart took a step backward. "And we owe Anderson something. He helped us win that pennant. Heck, if it wasn't for him, that trophy wouldn't be in your case right now, and you know it."

Erhart glanced over at the prize gleaming under the lights in the trophy case that took up a whole wall in his office. It was there with others the Rockets had won over the years. But there was one thing missing from the display as far as he was concerned. A repeat. So far none of the wins had been consecutive. And that's what he wanted most.

"That very well may be true," Erhart agreed, noticing the look of disgust on Tommy's face. "But I owe the investors, too. They pay the bills." He looked Williams in the eye. "And your salary."

"The heck with my salary. What's right is right and what you're going to do with Anderson isn't."

"I want to start spring training with a viable infield to let the other teams know we're set and we mean to repeat. If Anderson isn't ready, then he's going to have to sit out and let someone else play. It'll be Cabot's job to lose and the kid is hungry. Once he gets a taste of the big league, I don't think he'll be going down to triple-A ball."

"That stinks, Dick."

"We don't hold anyone's spot here, Tommy, and you know it."

"And that stinks more. All you care about is winning. Where's the loyalty?" Williams asked, his voice rising. "You want to go to Florida with a chip on your shoulder and line-up ready to put another a pennant in your pocket so you can wave it in front of the other owners' faces.

Yeah, it stinks. Like last week's fish, it stinks."

"Now calm down or you'll blow out that vein throbbing on your temple. It'll do the team no good if we have to replace the third baseman and the coach in the same week."

"What if I do quit?"

Erhart smiled, picked up his drink and took a sip. "Now Tommy, we both know that's not going to happen."

Williams raised his arms and let them drop to his sides. "Then there's nothing I can say or do to make you change your mind, is there?"

Erhart walked over to the picture window and looked out. With the field lights out, you could see the stars in the sky. "See those?" he asked, gesturing with his glass.

"The stars? What about them?"

"Every night some of those burn out and some others brighten." He turned back to Williams. "It's nature's way. And it's the way of baseball."


"What are you doing sitting in here in the dark?" Roger asked after he snapped on the light and saw Ryne in the recliner.

"Doing penance," Ryne replied, blinking and squeezing the bridge of his nose with his thumb and forefinger in response to the sudden brightness. "I'm running this whole thing over and over in my mind trying to decide if I could have done something to prevent April from agreeing to marry Tyler."

"You could have rushed in, grabbed the box and tossed it out the window."

"I don't think that would have endeared me to April." He leaned forward and rested his forearms on his knees. "You know the worst part? I think maybe he could give her a better life than I can."

"I think you could have given him a run for his money," Roger said before walking back into the office.

"Maybe," Ryne agreed. "But I lost my shot at the only person I think I will ever love. And I have no one to blame but myself."

He sat unmoving for a long moment, thinking about what he had and had not done. There was no doubt in his mind that the ache in his heart was going to be a permanent reminder that he had hesitated, and in that one frozen moment, he'd lost.

But maybe something good could come from the harsh lesson he just learned. Maybe that dull ache would help him make sure he never made the mistake of hesitating again.

He slapped his knees with his palms. "You know, Roger," he called out as he rose from the chair, "I've got a lot of work to do if I want to put this heartache behind me and get into the right frame of mind to start spring training with the team." He began heading for his bedroom. "I'll know better what I have to do after the meeting with the doctor in the morning. I better get some rest or I'll fall asleep on the treadmill."

As he passed the office door, Roger reached out and grabbed his arm. "You better read this." Roger gestured to the computer screen. "It's an E-mail from Tommy."

The look on Roger's face told Ryne whatever Tommy wrote was not good. "What is it?"

"You've got bigger problems than an engaged girlfriend, Ace," Roger replied, shaking his head. "You're out."

## Chapter Fourteen

The throng of reporters gathering in the parking lot of the Clinic blocked the entrance.

"Ms. Stevens, is it true Ryne Anderson's career in baseball is over?" one asked, thrusting a microphone bearing a sports logo at her face.

"When was the decision made to cut him from the team?" another shouted, reaching around the first reporter.

"Is he in there?"

"Can we get a statement?"

April shielded her eyes from the blinding lights of television cameras with one hand. Where did these people come from? How did they know?

"No comment," she said, pushing her way toward the door. "I'm sure the New York Rockets will call a press conference when a decision has been made."

"Does that mean Anderson can play?" a reporter asked, blocking her way.

She resisted the urge to knee him out of the way. "No comment," she repeated firmly as the sound of police sirens got louder.

The reporters turned to see a police cruiser pull up. "Ryne Anderson must be in there," one called out. They rushed the car as a group, shouting questions and encircling the car. It was the time April needed to duck inside the building.

Jenny met her at the elevator on the third floor. "This is not good."

"What happened?" She strode toward the conference room. She needed to talk to Ryne before the meeting started. She should have done it last night. What on earth had she been thinking?

"I'm not sure." Jenny matched her stride for stride. "Apparently there was a leak."

"Apparently." April's voice was laced with anger. "I know it wasn't you and it certainly wasn't me." She stopped just outside the conference door. "I have to explain this to him, if I can." She began to push open the door when Jenny put a hand on her shoulder.

"He's not in there." Jenny pulled the *Daily Times* out from under her arm. The headline on the back sports page was two inches tall, *Anderson Strikes Out*.

April grabbed it from Jenny's hand. "Ryne must feel like we've been hiding this from him."

"The story isn't good," Jenny added. "A lot of speculation on his condition and when and if he'll be playing, but they did get a vague comment from the team owner who confirmed that the Rockets' season probably will start without its premier star third baseman."

"I have to find him." April turned to leave, but Jenny stopped her. "Roger must know where he is."

Jenny shook her head. "I've been on the phone with Roger since I got here. There are a few sports reporters at his place, too, but Ryne isn't there. Roger said he left around midnight when an E-mail came in from the coach warning Roger what was about to happen. He thinks someone probably has been monitoring the team's E-mail system for some time and happened on this tidbit of information."

"Probably one of Wil's inventions," April groaned. "But that doesn't matter. What matters is that I should have told Ryne what I suspected about his knee earlier." April's shoulders wilted a little. She propped one hand across her stomach and dropped her face into the other. "I may be a good therapist. Maybe even a competent administrator. But I stink at knowing what to do when my emotions are tangled in with a decision I have to make. I wanted to do the right thing for everyone involved and it may have cost me the one person who meant the most." She shook her head forlornly. "Just like last time, I didn't come through for someone important to me." All of April's emotions grew spontaneously stronger. She squeezed the bridge of her nose with her thumb and forefinger in an effort to stop the tears that began to sting. Angry voices from inside the room made her snap her head back up. She looked at her watch. She was ten minutes late.

"You have to do this meeting," Jenny said firmly. "The press isn't going to go away until someone talks to them."

April let out a long breath of air. "I know. When I find Ryne, I'll need to be armed with facts and an action plan." She pressed her lips together and tossed her shoulders. "And with hope," she added just before she pushed open the door and went inside.

"For the last time, I don't know how the story got out." Dick Erhart slapped his hand down onto the cherry wood conference table so hard that the water glasses rattled. "But out or not, it's basically true. I don't intend to start the season without a solid infield and from what the doctor said, Anderson is going to need another six months to be totally ready to play." He turned to Dr. McKee. "That is what you've been saying, isn't it?"

"He could be ready in four. If he works hard," McKee conceded.

Tommy Williams began to speak, but Erhart silenced him with a swipe of his hand. "Tommy, we're not going to go through this again." He leaned back in his chair. "Anderson knew a critical evaluation was coming up right before the team heads to Florida." He swept his hand in the air. "And where is he? Couldn't care all that much if he isn't here."

April had enough. She rushed to Ryne's defense. "He cares and you all know it. He's been broadsided. He probably feels betrayed, too." She fought to control the heat she felt rise in her cheeks, feeling like she was the one who let him down more than anyone here.

She rose and walked to the front of the room. "Mr. Erhart, you've been talking about the business end of the problem." She turned to Werner. "And you've been strictly clinical. I've listened to both sides, and technically, I can't argue with either."

"What's your point then?" Erhart asked.

April sat down at their end of the table, a good view of both Dr. McKee and Dick Erhart, who were two chairs apart. The mid-March sunlight filtered through the blinds and lent energy to the conference room that fueled her strength of mind.

"I'm not a doctor, so there is no arguing with the medical aspect of this case, but I am a business owner, and in business, any business," she turned her head and looked directly at Dick Erhart, "there are smart ways to protect your assets and there are foolish ones."

Erhart raised an eyebrow. She had his attention. Fingers tightening around the pencil in her right hand, April gathered her swirling thoughts. In the next few minutes, she had to reduce Ryne Anderson to a commodity, devise a marketing pitch similar to the Nike Swoosh to identify Ryne Anderson and the Rockets as one, and then sell the package to Erhart.

"If Aaron McKee had to leave for a while, for whatever reason, sure, I'd have to find another doctor to cover his cases and schedule. But Aaron is the best." She looked at him and he nodded to her, acknowledging the compliment. "Any replacement would know the position was only temporary until Aaron was ready to come back. I'd be a fool to let someone like him leave just when Princeton Sports

Medicine is making a name for itself and trying to expand. Reputation can be a powerful motive for bringing clients to a facility," she continued, turning to look at Erhart. "Or putting fans in the seats."

She tensed, watching his features change as he mulled over what she said. No one was happy about this situation, least of all her. She felt like she muddled the whole course of Ryne's therapy, not working consistently enough or hard enough to keep his rehab on track. She'd let her feelings cloud her judgment, just as they had when her brother's career was on the line. She couldn't do anything about Rob's career now, but she fully intended to save Ryne's, even if it cost her own.

"You need to consider the consequences. Ryne's a popular player and the fans love him. You let him go and, once he's off the injured list, another team will snatch him up." April raised the stakes. "Maybe even your cross-town rivals, the New York Mets."

Erhart raised his hands in supplication. "It's a chance I may have to take."

"I don't think it's a necessary one, though."

"If you have another idea, I'm all ears."

"Dr. McKee has told you that Ryne could be ready in a few months if he works hard."

"Add to that a stint in the minors to get into shape. That will put us well into the season already," Erhart reminded her.

She turned to Aaron. "We talked about stepping up the rehab if we had to do so. You said it was possible for Ryne to be ready sooner. Maybe even mid-May."

"It would take a lot of dedication and determination. He couldn't do it on his own. Someone would have to devote a few weeks and almost twenty-four-seven to working with him to make sure he stays on track."

"Williams and I talked about this briefly. I can't afford to let the team doctor baby-sit Anderson. He and the team trainer need to be in Florida for spring training with the team. There'll be enough dings and dents in the guys from over the winter to keep both of them busy."

"I'll do it," April volunteered without hesitation. "We can work something out." With a quick intake of air, she watched Erhart react with puckered eyebrows.

"For a hefty price tag, I'll bet. Not to mention all the guys wanting this preferential treatment once they find out about it." Erhart shook his head. "And that would cost me a fortune in the end whether he recovers fully or not."

Don't think, April warned her whirling mind. Don't think of Ryne's incredible brown eyes, with long lashes that create thorny shadows on his cheeks as he smiled in the sunlight. Don't think about his touch caressing her skin, warming her heart as he brushed his knuckles along her jaw line.

Most of all don't think about how you probably love the man, his face, his gaiety, and his earthiness, the sound of his laughter, the arch of his brow. Don't admit that the time spent with him has a quality none other holds. No, don't think about any of that. Just do it.

After slowly releasing the breath she'd been holding she said, "If it doesn't work out, it costs you nothing. We both walk away. You just give Ryne an honest chance at coming back and making the roster, and I'll be satisfied we both held to the bargain."

Williams spun his chair to face Erhart. "Dick, this is one trade we need to make. You get the spot filled at third base when the season starts, Anderson gets a chance to win his job back, and I don't have to quit to make a point. Everyone wins." He straightened out the chair. He saw April watching him out of the corner of one eye and gave her a quick wink of approval. "Besides, we do owe it to him to let him try."

"But we still protect the team by starting Cabot," Erhart added. "And we let Anderson know his spot in the club is not a lock."

"I think he can live with that," Williams agreed.

Erhart rubbed his chin with one hand and tapped his pen on the table with the other. "Put it in writing, Ms. Stevens. I need to take it to our lawyers, but I think you can safely say that you have a deal."

After another few minutes of discussion, April watched everyone file out of the room. She sat alone in the large conference room with one more thing on her mind.

She needed to find Ryne before the media did.

## Chapter Fifteen

It was shortly before seven in the evening when she turned her car into the long driveway of the shore house and eased it to a stop next to Ryne's Audi. When she turned off the engine, she could hear the sound of the waves breaking onto the shore and gulls twittering in the distance. She wondered if Ryne had heard her coming over the natural shore sounds.

She didn't bother with the formalities of the front door, but took the deck stairs two at a time. The sliding door was locked, but she could hear Tammy Wynette belting out "Stand By Your Man" somewhere in the house and laughed at the irony.

She knocked but there was no answer. Pressing her head onto the glass, she cupped her hands around her eyes to better see inside. It didn't appear as though anyone was home. She would wait.

Turning, she walked to the edge of the deck and rested her hands lightly on the railing. The evening was clear, with a cool ocean breeze. The sky was a dusky blue. Behind her, the setting sun painted the horizon with reds, pinks and purples. Leaning forward, she scanned the beach. That's when she saw him.

About fifty yard down the shoreline, he sat facing the ocean. In the dimming light, she could see his arms resting on his knees and the muted angles of his profile. She watched as he picked up a shell from the sand and tossed it toward the water.

Slowly she walked down the steps, trying to rehearse what she'd say to him. Nothing coherent formed in her mind. This was going to be strictly ad-libbed.

At the bottom of the deck, she took off her shoes and stepped onto the beach. The sand was cold, but she didn't care. She stayed close to the dunes until she was right behind him, then walked forward and sat on his left.

He turned his head briefly to her and then looked back over the breaking waves. "Heck of a day, isn't it?"

"Pretty terrible," she agreed before casting a glance at him. He looked sad and very vulnerable. She tried to act as though every cell in her body wasn't begging her to touch him. "But it could have been worse."

He glanced at her again. "I suppose it could have. Some idiot could have taken a shot at America again."

April nodded and closed her eyes, feeling the sting of tears. "I hope never again."

"I agree. Things have changed since then. I've been sitting here thinking how I fit into the universe now and what

I can do to make a difference somewhere else, but I can't seem to find a place that makes sense. I lost something very important to me in the last two days, something I can never replace." He started to reach for her but then stopped.

April just looked at him for a long time. She could feel the heaviness between them, his fear and anxiety very real. She had caused so much of it by not telling him the truth when she first heard it from Dr. McKee. Again, she had hesitated. She wouldn't do it a third time.

"Reporters were swarming all over the Clinic this morning. The police chased them away, but an hour later they were back. Then, somehow they found out where I lived and camped out there. Now I know what a goldfish feels like," she said, digging her toes into the soft sand.

Ryne forced a smile. "They were at Roger's about midnight. I had to hop the back fence and cut through the neighbor's back yard to get away from them."

"So you came here."

"I had to sort things out. Not many people know about this place. I took a chance that the media didn't either." He turned his gaze back to the ocean and sat motionless.

For a few minutes, the only sound was the roar of the ocean. Ryne's silence ate at her. She felt such explosive emotions not knowing if he was going to hate or thank her when she told him what she had done.

She put her hands down behind her and leaned back, feeling barely coherent. Her heart hammered at the thought that she might lose Ryne forever if she didn't do this right. He wasn't a man who would accept pity or charity from her.

"I, um, did something." She leaned forward and put her right hand on his arm. "Something that is going to change things between us forever one way or another." Her other hand clenched and unclenched the sand. "And I want to talk to you about it."

Ryne looked at her hand on his arm and then up into her eyes. "Look, you don't owe me any explanations. I know what happened." He reached across his body and placed a hand over hers. Lightly massaging her wrist with his thumb, he managed a small smile. "It didn't work. You told me it wouldn't. I was the one who held out. I have to just walk away and not look back."

April pulled her hand free and, palms down, swiped at the air. "Wait. Something's not computing between us here."

"Ah, an aptly technical choice of words. I guess you'll be getting more into the swing of things with Tyler. But now that I'm unemployed, I won't be about to get you full twelve place settings of the Lennox, but maybe a starter set will be all right for the shower. For the wedding, though, it's pretty apparent that money is out of the question. What do you think you and Tyler would like?"

She waved her hands in front of her face. "What *are* you talking about? I came here to tell you that Erhart has agreed to let you have a shot at winning your job back at third base after you're fully rehabbed. You're talking like I've spent all day registering at Macy's rather than negotiating your return to the Rockets." She furrowed her brow. "How long have you been sitting out here? Have too many sea-gulls taken aim at your head?"

"Are you saying I'm back on the team?"

"Not exactly. You still have a bad knee and you're not cleared to play yet."

"But the papers said that Herb Cabot is probably going to be starting the season at third base."

"He can start. You can finish. But you and I have a ton of work to do before you can even think of that challenge. Then there's the time you'll have to spend at triple-A getting back into shape and showing Erhart you can still play. We really should sit down and map out a training plan as soon as possible."

Ryne pointed back and forth between April and him. "We? You. Me. Us? Won't that put a dent in the wedding plans?"

April scooted back in the sand so she could look him fully in the face. "Anderson, that's the second time you've talked about a wedding. Who is getting married to whom?"

Mouth open, eyes wide, Ryne slowly rose to standing. He motioned to April. "Get up, please."

Rising, she stood toe to toe with him. "Now what?"

"Show me your hands."

Palms out, she shoved them in front of his face. "You know, I really feel like squishing your face like a stress ball right now. This wasn't the reaction I expected."

Taking both of her hands in his, he lowered them to waist level and slowly turned them over. He brushed the damp sand from her fingers. "Empty!" he shouted. In one leap he slammed against her, nearly knocking her breath out while taking her against his chest. "You're not engaged."

She put her hand on his chest and stiff-armed herself

away from him as far as his arms would allow it. "No, but I am squashed."

"You're not engaged," he repeated. "Oh, babe, really?" But he didn't give her a chance to answer. He pulled her back and his mouth covered hers, wide and celebratory as he whirled them both in a circle.

When at last he stopped the spinning, she drew her mouth back to say. "Yes, really. What ever gave you that idea?"

He released her just a little. "I saw Tyler propose to you at the restaurant in Princeton. Then the crowd started clapping and you jumped into his arms."

"That was you who caused all the ruckus there?" Her smile grew as wide as center field. "I told Wil I thought someone was stalking the beautiful blond dining to our right."

"You were the only beautiful woman I saw that evening. A few moments ago when I told you I lost something important to me, something I could never replace, I wasn't talking about baseball, I was talking about you."

Ryne's beautiful eyes sparkled with the smile April loved, the one that half-closed them while his perfect teeth peeked out from behind upturned lips. When he pulled her closer to him, she wound her fingers into his wondrous wealth of hair. "We haven't even really begun on our adventure. How could you have lost me?"

He shook his head. "I thought you had agreed to marry Tyler."

"This is what was in the box." April arched her hair over her right ear and turned her head slightly. "Austrian crystal. Like them?"

Ryne kissed her cheek. "They look great." He trailed a series of kisses across her skin until he reached her mouth. "Really great."

While they kissed April's arms became a nest for his head, their mouths moving in impatient circles until they convinced themselves it was real. They heard voices in the distance, but they didn't care. They just kept on kissing.

Roger and Jenny, hand in hand, came flying down the deck stairs and ran onto the beach, coming up short at the sight that greeted them.

"Well, well, well," Roger drawled. "What do we have here?"

April's arms stayed locked around Ryne's neck while he craned around to look at his friend. Ryne's stayed around April's waist, unwilling to release her in spite of the interruption.

"What we have here," Jenny piped in, "is April telling Ryne about the deal she made with the Rockets."

"Does that mean she's going to join the team?" Roger teased.

"That depends." April kissed Ryne on the mouth, ending it with a noisy smack.

"On what?"

April's answer was drowned out by the sound of the back-up beep of a very large truck pulling into the driveway next to the beach house.

"What on earth is that?" Ryne asked, looking back as a tractor-trailer came to a halt at the edge of the sand, its rear lights illuminating the beach. An air horn sounded, scattering a few birds.

April broke free from Ryne's hold and began walking toward it. "It depends on whether or not I can bring a few people with me to the team. Come on."

Close on her heels, Ryne followed her. Halfway up the driveway, he stopped dead in his tracks when the truck's door opened and a pair of docksiders appeared on the running boards.

Wil Tyler grabbed onto the help bar and jumped down. He leaned against the truck's chrome bumper and emptied sand from his shoes. "Anderson. Good to see you, old boy," he said as the back of the trailer opened and two burly men began to unload the equipment stored inside.

"Hey, Mac," one called out. "Where do you want this stuff? We ain't got all night."

"I need the key, Ryne," April said, already up on the deck.

"Jenny and I left the front door open," Roger chimed in. "It'll be easier to get the stuff in through there."

Ryne threw his arms in the air. "Will *someone* please tell me what is going on?"

Roger slapped Ryne on the back. "Rehab, Ace. Yours. Here. Away from the reporters and with no one to save you." Roger pushed past him to direct the deliverymen to the front of the house.

Soon everyone was running in and out of the beach house except Ryne and Wil.

"How did you get involved in this?" Ryne asked.

Wil stood with arms crossed over his chest, the crest on his cotton shirt showing just over the monogram embroidery on the cuff. "April promised I could drive the truck.

She's quite a woman, that one." He looked Ryne straight in the eye. "And if you ever hurt her, I swear, the next truck I drive will contain your remains."

The house was finally quiet. April picked up a pair of ankle weights from the floor and put them on the shelf next to the sliding glass door. "Looks like a gym in here."

"I can't believe you did all this," Ryne replied, running his hand across some of the exercise equipment as he took a quick inventory of the room. He sat sideways on the leg press and asked one question. "Why?"

"I don't know," April said, walking to Ryne and brushing the hair from his eyes. "Funny things happen to women when they are presented with a challenge."

He pulled her onto his lap. "It's been a challenge since the beginning, hasn't it?"

"You felt it, too?"

He nodded, feeling his heart pumping hard, each beat slamming against his ribs. Now he was afraid for her. "I'm wondering. What if this doesn't work out? Wil told me you've put your career on the line for me."

"I guess that means you're going to owe me."

He ran his fingers through her hair, the strands soft and silky. "Ever since you told me what you did, I've been wondering what would happen if I failed and how it would affect you, because in turn, it's going to affect us."

April closed her eyes and rested her cheek against his forehead. Gently she ran her thumb across his cheek, loving the late-day prickly feel of his skin. "The thought of you failing never crossed my mind." She leaned down and placed a warm kiss on his mouth. "When I listened to Erhart talk, I realized they didn't know you the way I had come to know you. They only saw Ryne Anderson, the ball player, a commodity. But I know there is so much more to Ryne Anderson, the man." Touching his lips with her fingertips, she whispered, "And I love that man."

"I love you, too, April," Ryne said against her fingertips. "I think I've loved you from the day I met you." He moved her from his lap and they stood. He kissed her hair, her temple, her cheek. "I was so darn afraid I lost you to Tyler and there wasn't anything I could do about it. That's why I came here. Not to escape the thought of never playing again, but to escape the sight of seeing that ring on your finger at the meeting this morning."

"I wish I could have seen your face when Wil opened that little box in the restaurant," April said, snickering. "What a sight it must have been."

"I couldn't believe I had lost you to Tyler."

"Right now, there's something I can hardly believe," she replied.

"And what's that?"

"Do you realize that you haven't called him a computer chip all day?"

"Shh," Ryne said, silencing her with a kiss. He drew back and let his eyes caress her face. "I have something more on my mind than Tyler and his bits and bytes."

## Chapter Sixteen

"**T**wo hot dogs and two sodas." April motioned to the food vendor walking up the aisle at City Stadium. She handed him a ten and didn't get back any change. "Can you believe the prices here?" she asked, passing Jenny her food. She waved to Kevin Johnson, who as promised, was honorary ball boy for the day.

"Someone has to help pay for all that expensive rehabilitation," Jenny quipped. "As per your deal, the balance is now due."

"That's not why I did it, Jen. I believed in him." She sighed. "And I love him."

"Ya think?" Jen asked, a note of biting wit in her tone. "That was obvious to a whole lot of people long before you would even consider the possibility."

The tinny voice of the PA announcer cut April's reply. "And now the starting line-up for your World Champion,

New York Rockets." April felt her heartbeat rise in anticipation as the broadcast progressed. ". . . at third base and batting clean-up, Ryne Anderson."

Jenny put the tips of her forefingers between her lips and whistled like a longshoreman. April stood, clapping until her palms were red. They watched Ryne trot easily out to his spot from where they sat along the third base line.

"We're finally here," April said, sitting back down and watching him toss the ball around the infield in the usual pre-game ritual. "It's been quite an experience."

"You did it, girl. Now sit back and watch the fruits of your labor."

"We did it, Jen. You, me, Roger, Ryne and Wil."

"What a team."

At Ryne's first at-bat in the bottom of the first inning, on a full-count, he hit a two-run homer over the left-field fence. He jogged around the bases and April could see him scanning the crowd. She took off her baseball hat and waved it in the air, pleased when she saw him nod at her.

As he rounded third base, just as his foot hit the bag, he touched his fist to his heart and pointed at her, mouthing "I love you." She watched him jump on home plate, some of his teammates coming out of the dugout to congratulate him. April thought that there were no words invented to describe how she was feeling. She was sure that no moment on Earth could ever bring her greater pleasure.

In the dugout, Ryne accepted the high-fives of the rest of his teammates and stripped the batting glove from his hand. He walked over to the water fountain and took a long drink.

"Now that was a surprise," Roger said, sitting on the cement steps and nodding approvingly. "When did you acquire the patience to wait on an outside curve like that?"

Ryne tossed the glove into his batting helmet and stored it on the shelf above the bench. "I developed a whole lot of patience over the last few months."

"Nice shot. I think you shocked everyone in the stadium."

Ryne picked up his mitt as the batter after him swung and missed on a third strike. He tapped Roger on the arm with it as he walked past him to get back onto the field. "That's nothing compared to the surprise I have planned for later."

It was two hours post-game and the stadium was eerily quiet, nothing at all like the explosion of sounds and cheers after the last out with the Rockets winning the game when Ryne caught a screaming liner down the third base line for the final out. As April sat right next to the home team's dugout, she almost thought it felt like the calm before the storm.

But there was nothing to worry about. Physically, Ryne was stronger than ever. Professionally, he had just signed another three-year deal with the Rockets the day before. And emotionally, they were blissfully happy.

She heard the scuffing of his heels as he walked up the steps in the tunnel inside the dugout that led to the locker room. She stood and leaned on the metal rail. "Hey you," she said as he appeared. "What's all this cloak and dagger stuff and why did I have to meet you here?"

He folded his hands over hers as they gripped the rail. "I thought this would be an appropriate place."

"For what?"

Ryne ran his hands up her arms to her elbows. "In a minute," he cautioned. "Are you sure Tyler is coming in from Europe tomorrow?"

"He said he wouldn't miss the opening of the New York office," April said, touching her lips to his forehead. "But we both know what happened last time he promised he wouldn't miss a date with me."

"My luck, his loss, and . . ." He stopped and looked past her. A slow smile curled his lips and he let go of her hands.

April began to turn around when a voice stopped her cold.

"Is this seat taken?"

She closed her eyes, afraid to move, afraid to breathe. "Rob?" It seemed to take forever for her to complete the turn, but when she finally did, she stood face to face with her brother.

"Hello, April."

April's mouth opened, but no other words formed. Her gaze ran rampant over her brother's face as she registered ten years of change. His dark hair was shorter, his face thinner. Tiny lines fanned out from the deep blue eyes she hadn't looked into for over a decade. Slowly she reached out her hand and touched his arm. He seemed thinner, but he felt solid and real.

On the contact, he pulled her into a hug. "I'm sorry, sis. I'm so sorry. I've been so stupid. Can you ever forgive me?"

The tears she had been so carefully holding back broke free. She buried her face in his shirt and bawled like a baby. Her body shook with deep sobs, and she gasped from a combination of trying to stop crying and not wanting to.

Ryne jumped over the railing and peeled her from Rob's arms. "April, are you all right?" He tried to guide her into a seat. "Sit down before you fall down."

She pulled herself from him and threw her arms around Rob. "No. If I let him go, I may never see him again." She tilted her head and look back into her brother's face. "I've missed you so much. You're here. You're really here."

Rob planted a kiss on the top of his sister's head. "You can thank your boyfriend here for that."

Still holding onto Rob, she turned to Ryne. "You did this?"

He nodded.

"How?"

"He and some guy who looks like Bill Gates tracked me down in Arizona," Rob offered.

"Wil knew about this and he helped you?" she asked Ryne.

"He has all the computer connections," Ryne replied. "Once we found Rob, Tyler and I flew out to Sedona on Tyler's Lear jet and convinced Rob that he has a few fences to mend."

April's eyes grew even wider. "You and Wil? Working together? That's a small miracle in itself."

Ryne nodded again. "I know it somehow upsets the balance of the universe, but I wasn't sure what kind of resistance I would get. Roger and Jenny went too. I figured if we all approached Rob, he couldn't refuse."

"How did I not notice all of you gone at the same time? It's like one big conspiracy theory."

"You were busy setting up the New York office. It was a perfect distraction. I wasn't sure I could actually do it. I had no idea what I was going to say once I met your brother."

Tears crowded into April's eyes again. "I can hardly believe you did all this for me. Why?" Sniffing, she looked up into his deadpan features. Gone was the usual teasing. Instead his eyes were serious, somber.

"Because I couldn't think of anything else I could do for you that would come close to what you did for me," he said quietly.

April let go of Rob with one hand, careful to keep a handful of his shirt in the other. She touched Ryne's cheek. "I don't know what to say." She turned her gaze back to Rob. "It's like a gift I never thought I would ever get." She watched Rob smile and felt tears begin to trail down her cheeks. She finally released him and turned back to Ryne. "There is no way I could ever repay you for this."

Ryne brought his hands to her cheeks. His thumbs caressed her lips before he eradicated the distance between their mouths and kissed her gently, the touch filled with promise and love. "You can thank me by marrying me."

Her murmured agreement was lost in the reverb of the PA system. "Did she say yes?" It was Roger's voice. "Jenny and I want to know if we need to break into the champagne stash that Erhart has reserved for the World Series celebration."

Ryne, April and Rob all turned in unison and shot a thumbs-up toward the broadcast booth.

"It's about time," Roger said before he clicked off the mike.

"Go away, Roger," April whispered, lifting her arms and letting Ryne's close around her. His neck smelled of the aftershave she now knew so well. She held her cheek against the warm skin she found there and looked over her shoulder at her brother. She reached out one hand and, as Rob took it, she felt a sense of peace engulf her, a sense she had never felt before.

In the haze of joy that surrounded her, she looked forward to the future. Ghosts of the past were being laid to rest. She and Ryne had trusted one another to share their fears and dreams. And because they had, their reward was going to be a life together.

She had been wrong before when she said no other moment could ever bring her pleasure. Here, right now was the moment that would forever bring her the greatest sense of contentment and love. There was nothing more she could possibly want in her life. Ever.